STREE[illegible]
CONS[illegible]

Commander Altobelli sighed. He pushed the mugshots away from him and leaned back in his seat, staring up at the acoustic tiles on the ceiling. 'He's got us looking like jerks. Keystone Kops in the big city. Buffoons in blue. Who knows, maybe we deserve it. Maybe I've gone soft in my old age. I'm getting close to my pension, losing my instincts and trying to play it too safe. . . .'

Shaking his head in resignation, he opened the offending newspaper and stared dourly at the headlines on the front page of the metro section:

'Street Hawk 3, Police 0 . . . Again!'

In the same series

STREET HAWK

STREET HAWK 2:
CONS AT LARGE

A novel by Jack Roberts

Based on the Universal television series
'Street Hawk'

Created by
Robert Wolterstorff & Paul M. Belous and
Bruce Lansbury

Adapted from the episodes 'The Adjustor',
written by Nicholas Corea and
'The Unsinkable 453', written by Paul M. Belous &
Robert Wolterstorff

A TARGET BOOK
published by
the Paperback Division of
W. H. ALLEN & Co. PLC

A Target Book
Published in 1985
by the Paperback Division of
W. H. Allen & Co. PLC
44 Hill Street, London W1X 8LB

Typeset by Galleon Photosetting, Ipswich
Printed and bound by
Anchor Brendon Ltd, Tiptree, Essex

ISBN 0 426 20186 8

ONE

Jesse Mach drove his vintage Mustang into the parking lot behind television station KEIO, located a few blocks from Hollywood Boulevard and only a couple of miles from the police station. It was a typically gorgeous Los Angeles morning, with the air left clean by the previous night's Santa Ana winds, which had broken up a layer of smog that had been hovering over the city for much of the past week. As Jesse got out of the car, he spied a familiar VW Rabbit parked in a space reserved for TV personnel. A sticker on the back bumper read: OUR COPS ARE TOPS. He smiled wryly to himself, remembering the brainstorming session that had produced that slogan. He and Sandy McCoy had holed up in the Public Relations office back at the police station late into the night, sending out for Chinese food rather than disrupt their determined effort to come up with just the right saying upon which to launch their latest campaign to bolster the image of the Police Department, which had received a black eye in recent weeks as a result of several internal investigations.

Two particular bad apples had been uncovered – they had been using their badges as a pretext for waging a crime spree that rivalled that of most mob kingpins on either coast. It was Sandy who, in the midst of nibbling her last scrap of sweet and sour pork, had struck upon the slogan that now graced the rear bumper of her Rabbit. In trying to come up with words to rhyme with 'cop', she had dredged up memories of the old 'Sugar Pops are Tops' advertising jingle of her youth, and the rest, as they say, was history.

Carrying an attaché case, Jesse approached the guard post outside the entrance to the sand-blasted concrete bunker that served as the station's news facilities. He still affected a slight limp, ever mindful of the need to protect his *alter ego*. As he flashed his police credentials to a pot-bellied, blue-eyed security guard with a pencil-thin moustache, Jesse reported, 'I have some press releases for Miss McCoy. She's expecting me.'

The guard checked his clipboard to confirm Jesse's claim, then issued him with a visitor's pass and gave him directions to the newsroom, where Jesse found Sandy trying to read over notes for a noon newsbreak at the same time as a make-up man was dabbing at her face with a miniature pompom caked with flesh-toned powder.

'And how's my favourite anchorwoman today?' Jesse called out as he dropped into a chair across from Sandy and withdrew a file from his attaché case. 'Here's the latest on the Cummings and Dale proceedings,' he added, referring to new criminal counts being handed down against the two errant police officers.

'Thanks, Jesse,' Sandy replied, acknowledging her former partner out of the corner of her eye. 'I can't believe that after four months they're still unearthing more dirt on those two guys.'

'They sure had their fingers in a lot of bad business.' Jesse looked around at the newsroom, which was bustling with the activity of various crewmen readying for the next broadcast. 'I have to say, Sandy, this sure looks more exciting than working PR at the station . . . not to mention the jump in salary. Tell me, what do anchors on the six o'clock news make these days?'

Sandy grinned. 'Let's just say they made me an offer I

couldn't refuse. I miss the old job sometimes, though, I have to admit. How is everybody?'

'Fine, just fine. The Commander's started plunking Alka-Seltzer tablets into his Pepto-Bismol to keep his stomach from curdling, but other than that everyone's okay. Rachel's working out nicely . . . although no one can replace the great Sandy McCoy, of course.'

'Such flattery,' Sandy laughed, waving away the make-up man. As she picked up the press file Jess had brought her, she asked, 'Nothing new on Street Hawk here?'

Jesse shook his head. 'Why, should there be?'

'I don't know. I thought I heard something about the bike being equipped with some kind of high-calibre machine gun the last time it showed up.'

Jesse knew that it was a .50 calibre machine gun, to be exact. He'd put it to good use in busting up a smuggling ring that was using a travelling circus as a front for transporting cocaine and heroin across State lines. That had been just the latest in an on-going list of feats he'd performed astride the super-sophisticated motorcycle, disguised in a racing suit and designer helmet that shielded his identity from bystanders. There was only one other person who knew that Jesse Mach was Street Hawk, and that person wasn't Sandy McCoy.

'You know Altobelli isn't a big fan of Street Hawk,' Jesse told Sandy. 'The last thing he wants to do is publicize some upstart on a two wheeler who keeps showing up the Department.'

'Well, naturally the chief isn't going to blab about it, but that doesn't mean you don't have some information I can use on the air, right?'

Jesse smiled and shook his head. 'Sorry, but if you say anything on the air, he's going to know who your "informed sources" are. I may not be that crazy about my job, but I'd like to hold onto it until something better comes along.'

'Fair enough.' Sandy adjusted the collar of her expensive blouse and quickly checked her make-up in a hand mirror extracted from her purse. 'Well, I guess I'm ready for—'

A quick series of beeps sounded from Jesse's shirt pocket.

He reached and turned off the beeper, then stood up, apologizing, 'Sorry about that, Sandy. If you'll excuse me, I have a quick phone call to make. . . .'

'When did the Deparment start letting PR flunkies have their own beepers?' Sandy teased.

'Hey, I carry a lot of clout,' Jesse joked. 'Where's a phone I can use?'

Sandy pointed out at the hallway leading to the studio. Jesse excused himself and went to the phone. He didn't dial the station, however. The beeper wasn't his link to the Police Department. The signal came from Norman Tuttle, who was alerting Jesse that something had come up that would likely require an appearance by Street Hawk. When Jesse got through to the motorcycle's eccentric creator, he found out that, sure enough, a mission was in the making and he was to get on the bike as fast as humanly possible. The order was like music to Jesse's ears. . . .

TWO

In the heart of Downey, there were pockets of dreary inactivity in the midst of an otherwise thriving industrial climate. Along Firestone Boulevard, only blocks away from the heavily productive Rockwell plant, a row of abandoned factories stood idle under the beating sun, creaking now and then as a gust of wind blew past hanging signs and the unoiled hinges of locked gates. No one had been at work at any of these plants in several years, and aside from the ephemeral residency taken up by transients and bag ladies, the buildings were left deserted, awaiting either oblivion or a sudden, unexpected upswing in demand for the products that had once been put out by workers using the now dustladen machines that filled the echoing rooms.

A nondescript blue Ford sedan turned down an alley that ran behind the factories and slowly proceeded to the one unopened gateway on the entire block. Guiding his car into the parking lot, Mitch Elkins took a deep breath and stared at the large metal doors of the loading dock. His scheduled rendezvous was behind those doors, and when he reached them, he pressed his palm against the horn, giving off a sharp blast that echoed through the parking lot and made him jolt in his seat. He was a bearded man in his early forties, slightly overweight and dressed in an old suit that might have fitted him twenty pounds ago but now strained at the seams in an effort to hold his bulk. As he watched the overhead doors slowly roll open, Elkins chewed nervously at that part of his moustache that drooped below his upper lip.

'Hold your own, Mitch,' he muttered to himself as he drove into the enclosure behind the segmented door. The factory windows were boarded shut, and the only light filtering into the loading area was that which had followed the Ford from the parking lot. A rusted conveyor belt stretched out to the nearby loading dock, and an old forklift truck gathered cobwebs in the far corner, but Elkins didn't notice either of these things, because his attention was centred on the long brown Cadillac parked directly in front of him. The luxury car's front doors opened in unison, and two lumbering hulks climbed out.

Al Kirksey was two years older and thirty pounds heavier than his brother Tommy. Between them, though, they weighed a quarter of a ton and looked as if they might have a promising career as a wrestling tag team if they ever decided to get out of organized crime. Their suits fitted them perfectly, and they both had well-sculpted features . . . even if it looked as if some of the sculpting had been done by a switchblade in a dark alley.

Elkins felt his wee ration of mustered courage draining as he got out of the Ford and approached the Cro-Magnon bookends.

'You Elkins?' Al asked him.

'I'm Elkins,' the older man blathered. 'Yeah, I'm him.' His eyes were on the Kirksey brothers' right hands, which were stuffed in the pockets of their coats, obviously sharing the company of handguns. When Tommy and Al withdrew their hands and left the guns in their pockets, Elkins let out a quiet breath of relief. Al turned to the Cadillac and opened the back door, pulling out a hefty leather briefcase, which he carried over and dumped on the back end of the Ford.

'Okay, Elkins. Here's the goods.'

Elkins stared as Al unlocked the attaché case and sprang the lid open, revealing four separate compartments, each one covered with a hand-tooled leather lid.

'Neat little case, huh?' Al boasted. 'Picked it up during one of our heists . . . the same one where we got these babies. . . .'

When Al lifted the first lid, Elkins gaped at a trove of raw diamonds. Large, gnarled gems that could be cut into the kind of stones celebrity girlfriends liked to flaunt as proof of the devotion of their latest beau. Al dipped his meaty hands into the diamonds and stirred them about. Even in the dim light they glowed with the promise of wealth.

'Nice,' Elkins managed to mutter. His jaw was trembling at the sight of the jewels.

'Man, you ain't seen nothin' yet,' Tommy chortled. 'Show him the rest of it, Al. . . .'

'I plan to, Tommy,' Al sneered impatiently at his kid brother.

As Elkins watched on, Al opened the other three sections of the briefcase. One contained rubies the colour of blood and the size of eyeballs. Another was filled with emeralds of all dimensions, all vibrant green. The last compartment nearly overflowed with pearls, both black and white in hue and varying in lustre, all of them cultured to a perfect symmetry. They rattled under Al's touch as he poked his finger into the middle of the heap to demonstrate just how deep the filled compartment was.

'Pretty good score, huh?'

Elkins licked his lips, his mind reeling as he tried to grasp the street value of the haul he was staring at. 'Very nice,' he forced himself to respond nonchalantly. 'Quite impressive. I'd like to have a closer look, if you don't mind.'

'Why not?' Al chuckled. 'Just make sure you don't have sticky fingers, if you know what I mean.'

Tommy laughed along with his brother until Elkins reached into his coat pocket. Then they both fell silent and swiftly fetched their weapons. In what seemed like no more than the blink of an eye, Elkins found himself staring down the bore of two .357 Magnums.

'Easy, easy,' Elkins pleaded, slowly removing his hand from his pocket and showing the small box he had reached for. 'It's just a jeweller's glass. You don't think I'd be fool enough to try pulling a gun on you two, do you?'

The Kirksey brothers didn't lower their guns until Elkins had pried open the lid of his small box and revealed the small magnifying eyepiece inside.

'Never stick your hands in your pockets like that,' Al advised Elkins. 'We stay healthy in this racket because we don't trust nobody. Any false moves and we shoot first, then ask questions later.'

'I'll remember that,' Elkins said. He could feel his heart thumping against his ribs from the dose of adrenalin that had charged through his system. Under Al's close surveillance, he picked up one of the diamonds and held it beneath the jeweller's glass. There was a blue light that flicked on when Elkins pressed a switch on the base of the magnifier, enhancing his inspection of the quality of the gem.

'Look all you want. It's the real thing,' Al said. 'Everything in that case is the stuff we stole. Accept no substitutes!'

The Kirksey brothers snorted together like a stereo laugh track. Elkins nodded as he put the diamond back and turned his attention to a pearl. 'I have no doubts that this is the stuff you stole. My concern is just that some people store fake gems in their safes and keep the real stuff elsewhere. For what we're paying you, I have to be sure we're getting genuine merchandise. . . .'

'Well, check all you want,' Al said. 'Just don't take all day with it. We got better things to do than hang around a dump like this.'

'This won't take long,' Elkins assured the men. 'You'll be on your way soon enough. . . .'

THREE

Jesse was idling on Street Hawk in the shadowy alley across from the factory. Through his specially designed visor, he was able to see the three men huddled around the Ford inside the darkened enclosure of the loading area. He'd arrived on the scene moments before, after Elkins had already entered the factory.

'Everybody's here,' Jesse reported to Norman through his helmet microphone.

'I can see that,' Norman replied. Although he was physically miles away from the area, from his command module at Street Hawk's operational headquarters, he had a clear view of everything Jesse saw through the visor. The view was not clear enough to suit him, though. 'I think we need to make sure. Let me enhance the picture a little bit so we—'

'I can tell you right now, Norman, that it's the Kirksey brothers,' Jesse insisted. 'I've seen them in mugshots down at the station, and I know—'

'Enhancing,' Norman cut in, ignoring Jesse's interruption as he programmed his master controls in a way that magnified Jesse's view of the men gathered around the Ford.

Now he was able to make out clearly Elkins' features as he inspected the Kirksey brothers' stolen wares. Behind Elkins' back, Al and Tommy were trading conspiratorial glances.

'It's them, all right,' Jesse murmured, 'and from the looks of it, I'd say that Elkins is living on borrowed time unless I intervene. They're going to take him out once he's paid them off. I can feel it.'

'Then do what you have to,' Norman advised. 'But don't get carried away with the heroics.'

'Norman, you know I wouldn't do that.' Behind his visor, Jesse grinned as he started up his bike and rode out from the cover of the shadows. Instead of heading directly at the three men, however, he veered off to one side of the parking lot and approached a ramp that led up to the boarded windows facing the side of the building.

'Don't you dare, Mach!' Norman gasped, seeing what Jesse was up to over his monitor screen.

'Banzaiiiiiii!'

Jesse had noticed that the windows were covered only with thin layers of plywood, which easily gave way under the hurtling weight of Street Hawk. Crashing through the windows in a shower of glass and wood, Jesse landed a dozen yards away from the Kirksey brothers' Cadillac, bringing the bike to a sideway skid before stopping on the weathered concrete. He paused only long enough to make sure that when Al and Tommy drew their guns, they were going after him instead of Mitch Elkins. Elkins was one of the Department's most wanted men: an intermediary rumoured to be the link between Officers Cummings and Dale and organized crime figures, he was the one person who could bust that case wide open.

'Who the hell is that?' Tommy Kirksey wailed as he whirled around to face the dark-suited biker riding Street Hawk.

'Somebody who's gonna learn the hard way not to butt into other people's business!' Al roared as he drew a bead on the motorcycle and squeezed off a shot.

Jesse crouched forward and floored Street Hawk, lunging

to one side as he avoided the gunshot and headed toward the gun-wielding brothers. More bullets spat through the air in his direction, and when Norman witnessed Jesse's view of the warehouse, he cringed with anguish. 'Jesse, what are you doing!?? I told you to intervene, not commit suicide with my baby!!'

Jesse ignored Norman's complaining and concentrated on the way before him, whispering to himself, 'If they want gunplay, I'll show 'em gunplay. . . .'

'What? What did you say, Mach?'

'Watch, Norman. That's what you're best at!'

A volley charged forth from the .50 calibre machine guns mounted between the handlebars on Street Hawk. The weapon was currently the bike's main firepower, since the experimental particle-beam transmitter had been temporarily removed for more tests to improve its efficiency. As both Elkins and the two brothers dived for cover, bullets ripped into the Ford and the Cadillac, disabling both vehicles. The Cadillac suffered the most direct hits and was rent with a disfiguring explosion under the bonnet that shook the entire car. Shock waves, combined with the shower of hot lead pummelling the Ford, forced the attaché case on the car's boot to slide down to the ground. It landed on its side, spilling its treasures everywhere.

When Jesse was almost upon the battered vehicles, he activated Street Hawk's vertical lift system and jumped both the Cadillac and Ford. As Elkins and the Kirksey brothers stared with awe, Jesse repeated his flawless skid landing, stopping so that he had his twin mega-guns pointed at the three criminals.

'Hands up, all of you!' Jesse commanded through the visor, which effectively distorted his voice.

Al and Tommy had taken refuge behind their crumpled Cadillac, and they responded to Jesse's command by taking another series of potshots at him. Elkins, in the meantime, crawled across the concrete on all fours, desperately trying to gather up the fallen merchandise that had rolled across the ground. Jesse fired back at the Kirksey brothers with his machine gun, outlasting their ammunition and further obliterating their once-elegant automobile. When Tommy began firing on empty chambers, he reluctantly tossed aside his gun and raised his hands in surrender. Al did the same, cursing under his breath at Elkins, 'If you're the one behind this, you're dead!'

Elkins finished stuffing stray gems back into the brief-case, then looked over at Jesse, who ordered him, 'When I said to put your hands up, I was talking to you, too, Elkins!'

As he nervously complied, Elkins told Al Kirksey, 'I don't know anything about this! It ain't what I had planned. No way!'

Police sirens began to fill the air.

'Jesse, get out of there!' Norman commanded. 'Hurry, or you're going to box yourself in!'

Jesse glanced over his shoulder and could see the first squad cars already arriving on the scene, blocking off his most obvious escape route. Instead of going out through the main doorways to the parking lot, he turned around and powered Street Hawk up onto the conveyor belt leading into the main part of the factory. He rode past rows of untended assembly machines and a sea of empty work benches, then opened the throttle as he simultaneously triggered the vertical lift, catapulting himself through yet another window that led to the front courtyard of the factory. From there, it was relatively easy for him to vault the cyclone fence surrounding the front of the building and race past the other police cars speeding down the boulevard. Two of the cruisers tried to take up a chase, but when Jesse asked Norman to assist him in achieving a low-grade hyperthrust, Street Hawk quickly topped a hundred and seventy miles an hour, leaving Jesse's pursuers far behind.

'*Hi ho, Silver*,' Jesse muttered as he rode back toward LA's own downtown warehouse district. '*Away . . .!*'

FOUR

Jesse dropped Street Hawk off at Norman's warehouse headquarters and turned a deaf ear to the barrage of verbal abuse heaped on him by Norman for his reckless handling of the superbike. As soon as he had changed out of his racing suit and into his street clothes, Jesse bade Norman adieu and hustled to the police station, where Sandy McCoy's replacement, Rachel Adams, greeted him with typical exasperation.

'An hour and a half to drop off an info packet at the TV station, Jesse?' she said, her voice heavy with sarcasm. 'Did you travel by tortoise?'

'No, by snail,' Jesse retorted. 'Actually, I figured that while I was out I'd drop by City Hall and see if I could get any news out of the attorney's office on Dale's latest plea-bargain. His secretary kept me waiting for half an hour, then said Harris was called away on urgent business and couldn't see me after all.'

Rachel drew her slender fingers through her long hair and sighed, 'Well, I suspect that urgent business probably had something to do with a little incident that came down over in Downey. It seems we've managed to apprehend Mitch

Elkins, along with the Kirksey brothers. Harris probably figures that if he grills Elkins he can get enough info so that he won't have to cut any more deals with Dale.'

'Maybe Harris should hire Monty Hall for his assistant,' Jesse wisecracked. 'Now *there*'s a guy who loves to deal. . . .'

Rachel reached across her desk and grabbed several thick packets, which she handed to Jesse. 'Look, I know how much you like to spend your time on the road, so maybe you might want to deliver these parcels the rest of the morning. This bottom one goes to Santa Monica . . . if you stretch things out enough, you can have lunch on the beach and catch a little sun. You're looking a little pale.'

'You sound jealous, Rachel.'

'Nonsense. I love pushing pencils all days.' She rolled her eyes, then remembered something else. 'Oh, by the way, Jesse. Street Hawk was in on that bust in Downey, so you'd be wise to stay clear of the chief. He's in a royal funk, if you know what I mean. . . .'

Jesse nodded and started out of Rachel's office. He paused in the doorway and looked back over his shoulder. 'They didn't happen to catch Street Hawk, did they?'

'I just told you Altobelli's in the pits. What do you think?'

'That's one slippery biker.'

As he headed down the hall, Jesse smiled to himself. Although a part of him felt badly about constantly working apart from the police on Street Hawk, there was a certain undeniable thrill in his ability to always avoid being apprehended whenever members of the force showed up to finish his business. In a lot of ways, he felt as much like Superman as the Lone Ranger in the way he kept up a secret identity that allowed him to work side by side with the same people who found Street Hawk to be an upstaging nuisance. Of course, Superman had better public relations than Street Hawk, but Jesse Mach felt that he and Clark Kent were like two peas in a pod. If only Commander Altobelli knew that the notorious Street Hawk was lurking in the same departmental hallways he paced every working day. . . .

Jesse remembered Norman mentioning that he had

business to attend to in Ocean Park during the morning, and before leaving the station, he called Tuttle to arrange to meet for lunch at the Boardwalk Café in Venice. A chic eatery, the Café overlooks the beach, where now a choppy three-foot surf chewed at the shoreline and a few hundred sunbathers loitered on the white sand, playing with frisbees, reading pulp fiction, or just lounging in the heat and ogling at the tanned bodies that pranced about in skimpy swimsuits. By the time Jesse showed up at the Café, Norman had already been at a patio table for ten minutes and was resorting to sketching mechanical diagrams on a napkin to work off his nervous energy.

'Sorry I'm late,' Jesse said as he slipped into a seat across from Norman and promptly grabbed a menu.

'I'm used to it,' Norman grumbled. 'If you were ever on time, I'd faint.'

'That's what they say back at the office, too,' Jesse laughed. 'Gee, it sure is nice to work in an environment of positive reinforcement, let me tell ya. . . .'

A curvaceous bleach-blonde waitress came over to take the men's orders. Norman wanted soup and a pastrami sandwich. Jesse opted for a tuna melt, and when the waitress wandered off, he winked at Norman and said, 'Speaking of melt, she turns my heart to Jello. . . .'

'I'm not in the mood to hear about your love life, Mach,' Norman snarled as he opened a sugar packet and poured its contents into his coffee. 'You know, I had to patch up a few bullet holes in the bike thanks to your hotdogging in Downey this morning.'

Jesse yawned and looked away from Norman, eyeing a volleyball game being played on the beach a few dozen yards away. 'Spare me the lecture, Norman. I've heard it before and I know how it goes by heart.'

'Well, I wish you would take it to heart, then.' Norman stirred his coffee and took a sample sip, then added more sugar. 'You deliberately took—'

'—took unwarranted chances with a highly sophisticated piece of machinery, in which my government has invested—'

'—a lot of money, time and effort,' Norman concluded.

'Look, why can't you just do things by the book once in a while?'

'If you remember, dear Norman, I wasn't picked to ride Street Hawk because I do things by the book. It's because I'm a "hotdog" with the "right stuff". And, before you forget, let me remind you that Elkins and the Kirksey brothers are behind bars now, thanks to my "unwarranted chances with a highly sophisticated piece of machinery". . . .' Over Norman's shoulder, Jesse could see their waitress looking at their table and smiling. 'What's more, I think she likes you. . . .'

Norman was looking over the figures on his cocktail napkin as he rejoined, 'I'm talking about expenditures, not arrests. You have no qualms about running up the budget for our operation. If it's not repairs for the bike, it's luring me to expensive places like this for lunch instead of . . .' Jesse's last comment finally registered and Norman's expression suddenly changed. 'Wait a second. *Who* likes me?'

'The Venus of Venice,' Jesse told him. 'Right behind you.'

Norman blushed and reflexively took his glasses off for a moment so that he could clean them with his napkin. Then, summoning his nerve, he glanced over his shoulder. The waitress immediately drifted back toward the table as Norman recoiled in sheer terror.

'Hey, relax, Norman,' Jesse coached. 'Go with the flow.'

'Anything you need, sir?' the girl asked Norman.

'Uh . . . need?' Norman stammered. 'Uh, no. No, everything's fine. . . . Just fine. Thank you.'

'I'll have some coffee, too, please,' Jesse calmly requested. 'You can bring it with my sandwich.'

'They should be coming right up,' the waitress said with a smile. 'If you need anything else, just let me know. . . .'

'We'll do that.' Jesse waited until the girl was out of earshot, then leaned over and jabbed Norman on the forearm. 'Hey, playboy, you sure have a way with the ladies. Where do I sign up for lessons?'

Norman let out a groan of pent-up anxiety. 'Very funny, Mach.'

'Norman, when a beautiful lady like that asks you if there's anything you need, and you say "no", that's . . . that's a sin in my book.'

'Give me a break.' Norman's palms were sweating and he tried to dry them with his napkin, smearing ink over his hands in the process.

'You're a sinner, Norman,' Jesse pronounced gravely. 'Your only chance for redemption is to ask her out when she comes back with our lunch.'

'Don't be ridiculous.'

'Here she comes,' Jesse said. 'Go get 'em, Stormin' Norman. . . .'

The waitress returned with both men's orders. As she set Norman's platter in front of him, she commented, 'I like that sports coat. It's all wool, isn't it?'

'Yes. Yes, it is!' Norman ventured, opening the jacket to display its label. 'Worsted.'

'It's very nice. Can I get you anything else?' she added as she poured Jesse's coffee.

'I'm fine, thanks,' Jesse said. 'How about you, Norm?'

'Yes, I . . . I guess I'll have a refill of coffee . . . that is, if there's any left, heh heh,' he laughed nervously, noticing that her carafe was nearly empty.

'There's another pot brewing,' she replied cheerfully. 'I'll be back as soon as it's ready. In the meantime, enjoy your meal.'

Jesse kept a straight face and busied himself with cutting a slice of his tuna melt until the girl had left the table, then he looked over at Norman and taunted, 'When was the last time you had a date, Romeo?'

'None of your business!' Norman snapped.

'Well, let me give you a clue,' Jesse said. 'If you want to try the backhanded approach, just remember, they like the *strong* silent type, not the *wrong* silent type, got it? Trust me, a little bit of vulnerability goes a long way. In the past two minutes, you've used up enough to last a lifetime. . . .'

Norman shrugged off the jibe and sprinkled salt over his soup, regaining his composure. 'It just so happens I like to devote my free time to more important things than hustling women, Mach. Now, can we change the subject, huh? What about this Elkins guy? Is he a good catch for the Department?'

'I don't know yet for sure. He should be, but I didn't get a chance to talk to Altobelli about it. I guess the chief's a little miffed about Street Hawk being behind the arrests. I should know more this afternoon.'

'It would sure be good if they can get him to turn State's evidence against Cummings and Dale,' Norman suggested.

'That'll probably depend on which State ends up getting him,' Jesse remarked between bites of his tuna melt. 'From what I hear, there're warrants out for Elkins in ten States besides California. New York probably wants him even worse than we do.'

'Mmm, this is good soup,' Norman said.

'Maybe you could ask the waitress for the recipe,' Jesse suggested.

FIVE

Commander Altobelli had reached his limit of tolerance for the exploits of Street Hawk taking place in his precinct. He'd ranted and raved, fumed and boiled, paced and stomped – and he was no closer to apprehending the meddlesome upstart than he had been the first time Street Hawk had made headlines busting up a gang of liquor store robbers several months ago. The fruitless anger had taken its toll. Not only was his digestive system in a constant state of turmoil scarcely placated by the steady consumption of antacids and other medicinal supplements, but the fight had at long last been taken out of him. He felt tired and defeated, mired in a state of low esteem that seemed to be dragging him down like a bog of existential quicksand. Even the apprehension of three long-sought hoodlums in Downey failed to perk up his spirits, and as he stared at the newly-made mugshots spread out across his desk, he could barely muster the energy to sort through them.

'Alvin Delmore Kirksey and Thomas Gregory Kirksey,' he droned in a lifeless monotone. 'A pair of brainless dinosaurs in tweed suits who managed to duck arrests for a whole year after they weaselled out of the slammer on parole and jumped back into their old racket. . . .'

Rachel and Jesse were in Altobelli's office with the Commander. They looked at one another with concern. Neither of them had ever seen the chief this down before. As he flipped through the pictures, he continued to babble on as if he was by himself, talking in his sleep.

'And here's Mitchell Elkins, middleman fencer for the Kirksey boys' pretty stolen baubles . . . also middleman for two of our own Department's turncoats. My idea of a most wanted man. . . .'

'Ah, sir . . .' Jesse tried to interrupt, but Altobelli kept talking like a man in a trance.

'We log a thousand manhours trying to nap these three guys and come up with nothing, then along comes our local two-wheeled Zorro to do our jobs for us. They were all but gift-wrapped when we got to 'em at that factory, and Street Hawk's off riding into the sunset somewhere. . . .'

'We did everything we could to keep it out of the media, Commander,' Rachel said. 'It's just that all the reporters are always asking about a Street Hawk connection whenever there's an arrest these days. If we hold back, they go ahead and make speculations—'

'You don't have to tell me, Miss Adams,' Altobelli sighed. He pushed the mugshots away from him and leaned back in his seat, staring up at the acoustic tiles on the ceiling. 'He's got us looking like jerks. Keystone Kops in the big city. Buffoons in blue. Who knows, maybe we deserve it. Maybe I've gone soft in my old age. I'm getting close to my pension, losing my instincts and trying to play it too safe. . . .'

'C'mon, boss,' Jesse said, taking a step forward and smacking his fist against his palm like an over-eager salesman making a pitch. 'This isn't like you at all. You have to get this . . . this feeling out of your system before it poisons you any more. Yell. Throw something. Go ahead, it'll make you feel better. . . .'

Altobelli shook his head with resignation. 'I'm a little old for temper tantrums. Too damn old. . . .' He saw a newspaper on the top of Rachel's briefcase and grabbed it before she could see what he was doing. He opened the paper and stared dourly at the headlines on the front page of the metro section.

'Street Hawk 3, Police 0 . . . *AGAIN*'

The Commander's face flushed as his gaze remained fixed on the paper, which began to rustle slightly as his hands trembled from the trapped fury welling up inside him.

'Jesse's right, chief,' Rachel told him. 'It's not good to hold back those kinds of emotions.'

'Let it out, Commander!' Jesse rooted.

Altobelli suddenly launched himself to his feet and leaned across his desk, blaring, 'I don't need your damn psychoanalysis, Mach! Or from you either, for that matter, Miss Adams!' He furiously crumpled the newspaper in his fists and then hurled it across the room, where it bounded off the wall and landed a few inches shy of the wastebasket. The outburst served its purpose, however, helping the commander to shake off his doldrums and revert back to his old, cantankerous self. 'I'll tell you what I *do* need! I need to get my hands on that two-bit Road Warrior who keeps trying to show me up!'

'That's the way, boss!' Jesse cheered. 'Give 'em hell!'

Altobelli moved out from behind his desk and began to pace. Jesse sneaked a sidelong smirk at Rachel, who in turn flashed him a thumbs-up gesture to indicate that their prodding had succeeded. This was the commander they were used to dealing with.

'I'd like to get him in the ring . . . that's what I'd like to do,' the chief said, his eyes widening as he imagined such a confrontation. 'Eight ounce gloves. Just him and me! Miss Adams, did you know I was a Golden Gloves boxer once?'

'No, I didn't . . . sir.' Rachel tried to keep a straight face. 'I bet you were really . . . something.'

'Damn straight!' Altobelli grinned momentarily, giving the air a quick left feint and right uppercut. 'In my prime, I would have mopped up the canvas with this space cadet. Hell, I could still take him on, no problem!' He whacked his fist against the water cooler for emphasis, almost knocking the unsuspecting machine over.

'I bet you could, sir,' Jesse agreed. 'And, I have to say, you look like just talking about it has given you a good shot in the arm.'

'Yeah,' Altobelli grudgingly confessed. 'Maybe it has at that. . . .' He turned and glanced out through the glass partition that gave him a view of the main room, where everyone had stopped what they were doing to watch him. Raising his voice, he hollered, 'What do you think this is, a zoo? Quit gaping at my cage and get about your business! That's an order!'

As the others turned back to their various assignments, Altobelli poured some water into his coffee mug, then added an Alka-Seltzer tablet and a capful of Pepto-Bismol. Carrying the foul-looking concoction back to his desk, he told Jesse and Rachel, 'Okay, let's get back to business. . . .'

'Good idea, sir,' Jesse said.

'Now then . . .' Altobelli grabbed the mugshot of Elkins and said, 'New York's claiming dibs on our friend Mitch here. Extradition papers are being drawn up and they'll be sending out one of their own detectives to personally escort him back to the East Coast. When he shows up, I want you to make sure everything goes smoothly. I've got a deal cooking with the DA in the Big Apple, and if all goes well, they'll make sure to twist Elkins' arm, to get him to cough up the info we need to nail Dale and Cummings. Once I can close the book on those two bad eggs, I'll have my hands free to take care of Mr Street Hawk once and for all. . . .'

SIX

The stranger entering the station looked to be a likely donor in the event of either of the Kirksey brothers needing any spare parts. He was six foot three, not counting another inch of slicked-back hair framing a square-jawed face highlighted by a knob of fleshy nose that looked as if it had been broken more times than the four-minute mile. He wore a three-piece gaberdine suit that matched the ash-grey tint of his bedroom eyes. When he approached the nearest desk sergeant and produced a badge, the man spoke in a throaty baritone that carried as if booming out of a megaphone.

'Detective First Grade Vincent Cannon,' he announced. 'New York Police Department.'

The desk sergeant drawled, 'That's what the badge says, all right. You'll want to see Commander Altobelli. He's down the end of that hallway on your right.'

'Thank you, sergeant,' Cannon responded coolly, slapping his badge back in his pocket and taking the visitor's pass handed to him. He clipped it to the lapel of his jacket and marched determinedly down the hallway, his brogues thumping the linoleum with a steady beat. Reaching the squad room, he pushed through the unlocked door without knocking.

Inside the room, Officers Farnsworth and Holt were in the midst of discussing last night's football game with Bernie Goldberg, the bearded lab specialist. Holt was mimicking a quarterback as he told Bernie, 'The Forty-Niners had him trapped, about to make a rug outta him, so Plunkett scrambles out of the pocket and—'

Cannon entered the room and saw Holt backpedalling into him. Without bothering to warn the officer, Cannon shifted sideways and lowered his shoulder enough to catch Holt squarely in the ribcage. Taken by surprise, Holt reeled away from the blow, flailing his arms in a hopeless attempt to regain his balance. He bounded off the side of a nearby desk and landed seat-first on the squad room floor. When Farnsworth came over to give him a hand, Holt waved him away and bounded quickly to his feet, glaring at Cannon.

'Where the hell do you come off blindsiding me like that, ace?'

'You were the one about to slam into me,' Cannon said. 'You ought to be more careful . . . kid.'

Everyone in the squad room turned to witness the confrontation between Holt and Cannon, who was at least three inches and fifty pounds bigger than the man he'd knocked down. That didn't stop Holt from pressing his face close to Cannon's and shouting, 'Maybe I will . . . next time. And who do you think you're calling "kid"?'

'It's second and ten, officer,' Cannon warned Holt. 'I think you better pass.'

'Oh boy,' Farnsworth murmured from the sidelines. 'The fur's about to fly. . . .'

Before the altercation could escalate any further, however, Jesse pried his way through the other personnel and wedged himself between Holt and Cannon.

'Do you have business here, mister?' he asked Cannon.

Cannon raked the room with a look of disdain, then settled his sleepy eyes on Jesse. His voice was wide awake, though. 'Not unless you're Commander Altobelli.'

'I'm Officer Jesse Mach.'

'I don't need you. Where's Altobelli?'

'Over here,' the commander said, emerging from his office along with Rachel. When Cannon spotted Rachel, an odious smirk crept across his lips. Rachel sensed herself being undressed with Cannon's drooping eyes and she stiffened with anger.

'Which one of you?' Cannon coyly asked.

'I am,' Altobelli snapped.

As Cannon stepped away from Holt and waded through the other members of his department, he muttered under his breath, 'Hard to tell who's who around here. Whole place smells like hair spray.'

From behind, Holt called out, 'Coming from somebody who grooms with thirty-weight Pennzoil, that's real funny, pal.'

'All right, knock it off!' Altobelli bellowed. 'Both of you!'

Cannon removed a packet of papers from his coat pocket and handed them to the commander. 'I'm Cannon. New York Police Department. You're expecting me.'

Altobelli skimmed the papers and passed them to Rachel, then told Cannon bluntly, 'I gave my people orders to roll out a red carpet for you, detective, but seeing as you've got a way of tracking around mud wherever you go, I hope your only business is to pick up Elkins.'

'Metaphors aren't my strong suit,' Cannon said. 'Are you trying to make a point here or what?'

'My point is this, Cannon,' Altobelli barked. 'If all you need is Elkins, I can sign the papers and have you outta here with him in ten minutes. Planes leave for New York every hour. . . .'

'The quicker the better, Lieutenant,' Cannon replied.

'It's Commander, Cannon. And you can bet it'll be quick. Mach! Take Detective Cannon over to Processing so we can turn Mr Elkins over to him.'

Jesse glanced over at Farnsworth and rolled his eyes. 'I had a feeling he was going to say that. . . .'

Neither Jesse nor Cannon spoke as they walked to the other side of the building. Altobelli had already called ahead with the okay to release Elkins, and the processing ritual was already in motion. The prisoner looked as if he hadn't slept since his arrest, although his suit was now rumpled so much it seemed that he must have worn it in place of pyjamas. He stared bleakly at the formica counter as the attending officer emptied out a large envelope filled with his confiscated belongings. Jesse and Cannon both had to sign release forms before Elkins could transfer the goods into the pockets of his suit, then the sergeant pressed a buzzer, allowing a door in the counter to swing open. Elkins stepped forward reluctantly and Cannon unclipped a pair of handcuffs from his waist. Jesse watched uncomfortably as the detective slapped the cuffs on Elkins, then shoved him toward the exit.

'There's no need to rough him up, Cannon,' Jesse finally said, deciding there was only so much he could tolerate, regardless of Altobelli's earlier orders to accommodate Cannon.

'Don't sweat the small stuff, Hollywood,' Cannon told Jesse as he herded Elkins out into the hallway. 'This is New York business now. He's my prisoner. You got that?'

'I didn't say he wasn't, Cannon,' Jesse retorted. 'It's just that there are certain ways of doing things that you don't seem to be considering.'

'For instance?'

'For instance, out on this coast, police brutality isn't our basic way of dealing with prisoners.'

'Yeah!' Elkins blurted out miserably. 'I'm going to sue on account of police brutality!'

'Shut up, Elkins!' Cannon ordered, giving the prisoner another shove. 'You don't want to know what real police brutality is, New York style!'

'Back off, Cannon,' Jesse warned, blocking the detective's way in the hall. 'I don't want to have to tell you again.'

'What's it to you anyway, Hollywood?' Cannon griped. 'You act like you busted this guy yourself or something.'

Jesse checked his temper, then stepped aside to let Cannon pass. 'We better get you out of here before you miss your plane.'

'Don't worry,' Cannon chortled. 'There's one every hour, remember?'

SEVEN

Over Cannon's objections, Jesse accompanied the detective and his prisoner to LA International Airport, driving them in his Mustang. Little was said during the entire trip, which suited all parties. Cannon was bristling with visible impatience, while Jessie was wary of Elkins' fate once he dropped them off at the terminal. Elkins himself was clearly terrified of being left alone with Cannon, and as Jesse weaved through airport traffic and parked at the curbside in front of the Eastern Airlines terminal, the prisoner pleaded, 'Are you sure you can't just come in and see me off?'

Jesse shook his head. 'Sorry, Elkins.'

'Quit your whining, Elkins,' Cannon said as he got out of the Mustang and held the door open. 'There's thousands of people around here, so you don't have to worry about a thing unless you force my hand.'

'What about my handcuffs?' Elkins said.

'What about them?'

'Aren't you going to take them off? Come on, give me a little dignity, would you?'

Cannon leaned over and sneered at Elkins. 'You taken a good look at yourself lately, schmuck? You look like a slob, so don't give me any of that crap about dignity. Now get outta the car before I have to drag you out!'

As Elkins was wriggling out of the back seat, Jesse turned to him and whispered, 'If you know what's good for you, you'll mind your manners and play ball with the DA once you're in New York. He can help see to it that you do time here instead of on the East Coast.'

'You think you're my lawyer or something?' Elkins sniffed. 'Listen, I know how to handle myself. As long as King Kong here doesn't rip me apart before I get to New York, I'm gonna talk my way outta doing any time, period. Dig?'

'Good luck,' Jesse told him. 'You're sure as heck going to need it.'

Jesse drove off and Cannon escorted Elkins through the crowd into the terminal, drawing stares from people who noticed that the prisoner's hands were cuffed behind his back. By flashing his credentials at a security guard, Cannon was able to cut through the long lines at the ticket desk and secure reservations on the next flight leaving for New York, which was scheduled to depart in thirteen minutes.

'Thirteen, huh?' Cannon sniggered at the ticket clerk. 'That's my lucky number.'

The clerk smiled stiffly as she eyed the abject figure of Mitch Elkins. 'Have a nice flight,' she offered.

Once they had passed through the metal detectors, Cannon led Elkins down a long hallway leading to the airline's arrival and departure gates. Pedestrian traffic was thin along this stretch, and when he guessed there were few people watching, Cannon suddenly grabbed Elkins by the arm and hauled him to a janitorial supply room. No one else was in the cramped quarters, and Cannon quickly tracked down a broom which he stuck through the door handle in such a way that made it impossible for anyone to get in.

'Hey, what's going on?' Elkins wanted to know.

'I just figured you'd want to get comfortable,' Cannon said as he unlocked the other man's handcuffs. 'There, how's that?'

'Great,' Elkins replied suspiciously, rubbing his chaffed wrists. 'Thanks, but why—'

Elkins was cut short when Cannon's right fist came crashing into the side of his head, spinning him into a row of metal lockers. He slumped to the floor, moaning as he reached for his throbbing jaw. The blow had nearly knocked him out, and when Cannon grabbed him by the lapels and jerked him to his feet, Elkins was barely able to stand up. Cannon helped him by pinning him against the wall.

'W-w-what did you d-d-do that for?' Elkins' teeth were swimming in blood, making it hard for him to talk.

'To get your attention,' Cannon told him. 'Now let's talk about Mr Girard's money.'

Elkins blinked the stars out of his eyes and blubbered, 'Who?'

Cannon snapped his prisoner's head to one side with the back of his hand. 'Wrong answer, punk. Try again!'

'I . . . don't understand,' Elkins said feebly. 'What's Girard got to do with this? That's not why I'm going to New York. . . .'

'You aren't going anywhere unless you fork over the money Girard fronted you for those goodies you were supposed to buy from the Kirksey brothers. Five hundred grand. Am I making myself clear, Elkins?'

A horrible truth dawned on Elkins, and the presence of the man in front of him became suddenly more ominous. 'You,' he muttered. 'You're not a cop. . . .'

'Good guess, Einstein.' Cannon let go of Elkins and took a step back, removing his pistol from a shoulder holster beneath his jacket. From one of his coat pockets he also withdrew a silencer. As he fixed it to the barrel of his gun, he told Elkins, 'Why don't you stay smart and let me know where that money is. They didn't find it on you when they arrested you. You haven't spent it already, have you?'

'No, no,' Elkins said, dabbing blood from his mouth with the sleeve of his jacket. 'I haven't spent it.'

'That's good. Maybe you've just saved your life.'

'I . . . I'll tell you where it is,' Elkins bartered.

Cannon shook his head. 'No, Elkins. I have a better idea. Why don't you show me?'

'Sure,' Elkins spluttered. 'But what about our plane?'

'I guess we'll just have to refund our tickets, won't we?' Cannon tucked his gun inside the waistband of his pants instead of the holster, then removed the broom from the door handle. 'Okay, let's go. And just remember one thing. I get my fee from Mr Girard whether or not I come up with the money, so I got no qualms about putting a few holes in you if you try anything. Savvy?'

Elkins nodded, but he took secret hope in the fact that Cannon hadn't bothered to reapply the handcuffs before leading him out of the supply room. They began back-tracking away from the departure gate, and Elkins forced himself to ignore the piercing headache that had come to him in the wake of the blows Cannon had dealt him. He concentrated on his surroundings, looking for an opportune moment. There was no doubt in his mind that he was a dead man unless he got away from Cannon, and he wasn't going to have a better chance to make his move than in the terminal. The closer they got to the exit, the more crowded the hallway became, but Elkins still didn't think it was safe enough. He waited until they had passed the security station and were heading for the ticket counters. Then he spied a red cap lugging a pushcart piled high with luggage directly toward them. When the uniformed cap was passing next to Cannon, Elkins sprang into action.

With a loud exclamation, the prisoner veered sharply to one side and shoved Cannon with all his might. Cannon toppled into the luggage cart and tumbled to the floor as the wall of Samsonite gave way under his teetering weight.

Charged with fear, Elkins sprang in the other direction, shoving people out of his way as he tried to put as much distance as possible between himself and his would-be executioner.

'You'll pay!' Cannon raged as he pried himself loose of the fallen luggage and jumped to his feet. When the irate red cap began to argue with him, Cannon whipped out his gun and pointed it at the other man's face. 'You want a lead lobotomy?'

The red cap shrank away from Cannon, who charged past

him and began cleaving his way through the riled crowd, knocking down anyone in his path as if he were an All-American fullback trying to nail down the Heissman Trophy. By the time he caught sight of his prey, Elkins had reached the security station and was nonchalantly passing through the metal detector a second time. Once he had cleared the detector, Elkins chanced a glance over his shoulder and saw Cannon in hot pursuit. With lengthening strides, Elkins wormed his way into the throng of passengers heading for the terminal gateways.

Mindless of anything but catching up with Elkins, Cannon bowled over several more people, then set off the alarms on the metal detectors as he rushed through one of the booths.

'Hold it right there!' a security guard shouted, whipping out his own pistol and aiming it at Cannon. A second officer did the same.

'I'm a cop, dammit!' Cannon shouted, reaching for his shirt pocket. 'I'm after an escaped prisoner, and if you don't let me—'

'Keep those hands up, pal!' the second security guard commanded as he moved forward.

'But he'll get away!' Cannon protested.

The first guard snatched Cannon's gun from him.

'Why don't you let us worry about that, hmm?'

'Idiots!' Cannon raged. 'I'll have your badges for this!'

'If you don't cool down, fella, it's gonna be the other way around,' the second guard warned Cannon. 'This isn't a damn shooting gallery. . . .'

EIGHT

An hour after Mitch Elkins' escape, Detective Cannon was back at the police station, still hot under the collar. He'd given his taxi driver such a rough time on the ride from the airport that the cabbie followed him into the station to file a complaint while Cannon was ushered into Altobelli's office. Jesse was there, too, and he was hardly surprised when he heard Cannon relate a selectively edited version of the events that had transpired after Jesse had dropped him and Elkins off at the airport.

'. . . and I would have got him, too,' Cannon concluded, pacing in such a wide circle that Altobelli was pinned behind his desk and Jesse had to lean against the wall by the water cooler to keep from being inadvertently sideswiped. 'But those moronic rent-a-cops started waving artillery at me like *I* was the bad guy, and—'

'You had your piece out, Cannon,' Altobelli calmly reminded the detective. 'They had no way of knowing you were a cop.'

'Damned right I had my piece out!' Cannon spat. 'And I would have dropped that little creep if—'

' "Dropped" him?' Jesse interrupted, amazed at Cannon's

gall. 'You would have fired? In a crowd that size?'

Cannon stopped pacing, caught momentarily off-guard by the accusation. He licked his lips, then threw his arms up in exasperation. 'Well, probably . . . no, of course not. I'm just teed off, that's all. No, I wouldn't shoot in a crowd.'

Neither Altobelli nor Jesse were convinced, but they didn't press the matter. Jesse instead asked, 'Why'd you uncuff Elkins in the first place?'

'I didn't think he'd have the guts to make a break for it.' Cannon's temper faded briefly and was replaced by a fit of nervousness. He resumed pacing. 'I don't know. . . . I guess I just didn't want to embarrass him with the cuffs and all. Criminal or not, I figured he was entitled to a little dignity.'

'That's not what you were saying when I dropped you two off,' Jesse insisted. 'I think you ought to get your story straight, Cannon. . . .'

Cannon spun about and took a threatening step towards Jesse, who moved away from the wall, ready for a face-off.

'Cool it, Cannon!' Altobelli shouted from his desk.

Cannon and Jesse locked gazes for several seconds, then the detective turned away, taking out his frustration on Altobelli. 'Look, the bottom line is Elkins got away and according to the airlines he didn't fly out of there, so he's gotta be on the loose around here! If your men were competent he'd already be apprehended!'

'Don't you lecture me about competence, detective!' Altobelli rose from his seat and pointed an accusatory finger at Cannon. 'I've got APBs on the street and his picture's being circulated. A whole lotta manpower being used up on account of your screwing up! And don't you forget it!'

Cannon was about to shout back at the commander, but he held himself in check, thinking better of it. There was a moment of uneasy silence in the cubicle, then Cannon nodded grimly and let out a sigh that seemed to exorcise him of his fire and brimstone. 'Listen, Commander. I apologize. Like I said before, I'm just kinda teed off, you know? I got this reputation of being New York's answer to the Royal Canadian Mounted Police . . . I always get my man. Only this time, like you say, I screwed up. It was my fault, no more excuses.'

'That's more like it,' Altobelli said, relaxing.

'And I owe you an apology, too,' Cannon told Jesse.

Jesse stared dubiously at the detective, then shrugged his shoulders. 'Everyone blows a fuse now and then, I guess.'

Appealing to both of the local men, Cannon went on, 'I want to give you guys a hand in recapturing Elkins. It's the least I can do.'

Jesse clearly expected the chief to turn down Cannon's offer, and he was shocked when he saw Altobelli nod his head. 'We'll work something out, Cannon.'

'Good. I'm going to get some air, wash up. I'll be back in a few minutes.'

Altobelli dropped back into his chair as Cannon left the room. Jesse quickly strode over to the desk and confronted his boss.

'You can't be serious, chief, that guy—'

'Quiet, Mach!' Altobelli held a hand as if he was ready to stiff-arm Jesse. 'Look, I talked to New York, and as far as *his* boss is concerned, Cannon can do everything but walk on water . . . and maybe even that.'

Jesse shook his head miserably and snorted, 'Right, okay . . . so he's just "out of his familiar element" here, that's all. He's not normally like this. In real life, he's a swell, wonderful guy who runs an orphanage in his spare time. Sure . . . and I'm Mahatma Ghandi.'

Refusing to be ruffled by Jesse's sarcasm, Altobelli corrected, 'No, you're Detective First Grade Vincent Cannon's temporary partner.'

'What!?'

'You heard me.' Altobelli stirred his ever-present mug of pink brew and took a long sip, making a face that rivalled Jesse's for unpleasantness. Then he told Mach, 'The sooner we find Elkins, the quicker we send Cannon back to his "familiar element" . . . and out of ours.'

'Boss, in case you haven't noticed, I have big problems with this guy. And he has big problems with me.'

'Life is full of big problems, Mach. Get used to it.'

'There's more to it than that,' Jesse insisted. 'This Cannon just isn't . . . right. Know what I mean?'

Altobelli had a pile of paperwork awaiting his attention and he started sifting through it. Without looking up, he told Jesse, 'Be specific or button up.'

'It's a feeling. Like intuition.'

The commander drummed his fingers impatiently on his desktop. 'Psychics have intuition, and I don't believe in psychics.' Altobelli stared at Jesse and started counting his fingers. 'Let me explain some elementary logic to you, Mach. One . . . you have a job to do. Two . . . if you do that job well, then my job is easier. Three . . . if my job is easier, then your life is easier. Four . . . if your life is easier, everyone's a winner. And five . . . you've got five seconds to get outta my sight and start taking care of business.'

'I hear you, chief.' Jesse turned and headed for the door. As an afterthought, he added, 'What do I do if he gets out of line?'

'Don't ask me foolish questions, Mach. I'm putting you with him so that he *will* stay in line. *Comprenez-vous?*'

'*Oui,*' Jesse conceded, 'I'm afraid so.'

Jesse found Cannon in the back corner of the squad room, where he was inflicting his wolfish charm on Rachel.

'So, anyway, since I might be in town a couple of days longer, I thought maybe you and I could get together for some dinner and a show somewhere. . . .'

'I'm flattered, detective,' Rachel said, looking over Cannon's shoulder at Jesse like someone seeking relief. 'However, I'm also spoken for.'

'Hey, it's not a marriage proposal, for cryin' out loud,' Cannon chuckled. 'You'd just be showing some hospitality to an out-of-towner. . . .'

'Unless I'm mistaken, Cannon,' Jesse cut in, 'you're here on business, not to fill out a social calendar. Let's hit the streets.'

Cannon shot an angry glance at Jesse, then turned back to Rachel. 'At least keep it in mind. It shouldn't take me too long to get my mitts on Elkins . . . provided that Goody Two-Shoes here gives me room to move.'

'Ah . . . if you'll excuse me, gentlemen . . .' Rachel drifted out of the squad room, leaving the two adversaries.

'Look, Cannon,' Jesse said as he pointed to the rear exit across the room. 'We'll take my car. As long as we're stuck with each other, why don't we hold the verbal abuse to a minimum and try to make things as painless as possible, okay?'

'Suit yourself . . . but I was under the impression that you were strictly a PR man,' Cannon said as they crossed the squad room and headed down a set of stairs leading to the back parking lot.

'I put in my share of time on the street,' Jesse said. 'I was a bike cop until I had an accident and messed up my knee.'

'Tough break.' Cannon lit a cigarette and blew smoke.

'That's life in the big city. The chief still puts me on assignment whenever he can get away with it. He knows I'd go crazy if all I did was shuffle papers all day.'

The men got into Jesse's Mustang and left the station, heading crosstown. Jesse couldn't stand the smoke wafting in his face from Cannon's cigarette, but he didn't want to start anything by asking him to put it out. As they got on the westbound freeway, Cannon stared out at the sprawling city and wondered aloud, 'We got our work cut out for us. Hell, this town's spread out all over the place. We're talking needle in a haystack. . . .'

'Maybe not,' Jesse countered, weaving through traffic. 'We know that both Elkins and the Kirksey brothers spent a lot of time around Ocean Park and Venice. Elkins in particular rented a flat near Rose Street. It's already been cleared out and rented to someone else, but it'd be worth our while to check around the area and see if anyone's spotted him since he jumped. It's only a few miles from the airport, after all. . . .'

'It's your city,' Cannon said, stubbing out what was left of his cigarette and lighting up a fresh one. 'As long as we get him, I don't care how we do it.'

'That's what I figured you'd say. . . .'

NINE

The apartment complex off Rose Street where Mitch Elkins used to hang his hat was an old stucco affair, two stories high and surrounding a drab courtyard that had more dirt than grass and only a few spindly plants growing in the planter area. A handful of children were playing ball in the courtyard as Jesse and Cannon entered the complex, and they all paused to gawk momentarily at the new arrivals. Jesse smiled at the kids and waved, but Cannon scowled past them, eyeing the door numbers of the various apartments. There were only a dozen units, so it was easy to track down Elkins' former digs. An old woman was sitting in the doorway of apartment eight, knitting as she glanced down at the children.

'Let me talk to her,' Jesse said, removing a xerox copy of Elkins' photo from his shirt pocket. 'Why don't you see if you can track down the manager. He's in number one.'

'Right.' Cannon swaggered past the children, telling them, 'What's the matter, you never seen a grown-up before? Go back to playing your game already!'

The youngsters resumed their play as Cannon knocked on the apartment manager's door and Jesse headed up the steps to the second floor. When he approached the old woman, he put on his best public relations smile and called out cheerfully, 'Hello, ma'am! How are you this fine day?'

'Don't patronize me, sonny,' the woman snapped, squinting her small eyes as she peered up over her bifocals at Jesse. 'If you're selling something, I'm not interested, and if you're thinking of trying something funny, I still got a good set of lungs and I'll scream so loud your ears will spin.'

Jesse saw further that the woman was now clutching her knitting needles like lethal weapons, and he held his hands out to his sides in a gesture of appeasement. 'Ma'am, I don't mean any harm, and I'm not selling anything. I'm with the police. We're looking for a man who used to live in this complex. Here's his picture. . . .'

The woman, who looked as if she weighed no more than ninety pounds, suddenly lashed out with one of the knitting needles, stabbing the flyer. Jesse let go of it and she retrieved it, then held it out so that she could get a better look at Elkins' face.

'Ugly man, isn't he?' she remarked.

'You'd know it if you'd seen him, then,' Jesse suggested.

'Maybe, maybe not, but I don't recall seeing him around here. Of course, I'm new to these parts. Just moved in, you know.'

'Yes, ma'am,' Jesse replied. 'Well, can you do me a favour and keep that flyer? If you *do* see that man, there's a number on the bottom of the page for you to call. We'd sure appreciate your help.'

The woman stuffed the flyer in a knitting bag near her feet, then put her elongated needles back to their intended purpose. A hint of a smile finally came over her wrinkled face as she apologized, 'Sorry to be such an old witch, young man, but like I say, I'm new here and I don't want to be taken advantage of. I used to be a school teacher, you know, and it was always our philosophy that if you were nice to students the first day, they'd take advantage of you the second day and the rest of the year would be just as bad.'

Jesse smiled back at the woman. 'Now I know why *my*

teachers were always so gruff the first day of school. Well, good day to you, and sorry about the disturbance.'

'Nonsense,' the woman scoffed. 'I'm always glad to help the police. What goes around comes around, you know? There might be a time when *I* need some help. . . .'

'If you ever do, you make sure and call the station and tell them you know Jesse Mach.'

'Why, thank you, young man! Jesse . . . that's a nice name, as long as you don't think of Jesse James, of course!'

The woman laughed to herself and Jesse nodded, then turned around and headed down the steps. In sharp contrast to his positive reinforcement, Detective Cannon was using a different strategy on the children. He'd intercepted their ball and was holding it over his head so they couldn't reach it.

'Okay, if you want your ball back, all you have to do is tell me all you know about this guy in the picture I'm holding, okay?'

The children stood around Cannon silently, staring at both their ball and the mugshot of Elkins.

'Come on, I know you've seen this guy around!' Cannon snapped. 'Let's have some answers, okay?'

Clearing the bottom step, Jesse crossed the courtyard and batted the ball out of Cannon's hand before the detective could react.

'They're just kids, Cannon! Leave 'em alone!'

Cannon took a long step forward and glared down at Jesse, sneering, 'You trying to make me look bad?'

'No, I'd say you're doing a good job of that all by yourself!'

One of the kids retrieved the ball while another stepped forward and told the men, 'That's Mr Elkins. He used to live here, but he doesn't any more. He moved out.'

Jesse asked the youth, 'And he hasn't come back? Not today especially?'

'No, sir.'

Jesse told the kids that if they did see Elkins, they should report to the old woman upstairs, who overheard his directions and shouted her approval. As Jesse and Cannon headed back to the car, the detective said, 'The apartment owner says Elkins skipped out owing back rent, so it's not likely he'll be showin' his face around here.'

'Then we'll just have to start looking elsewhere,' Jesse said, getting into his car, 'and I hope you can start using a little more tact. This isn't New York. You can be polite and still get results.'

Cannon lit up another cigarette as he slipped into the front seat. 'Mister Public Relations,' he muttered bitterly. 'I can see this is going to be one long day. . . .'

TEN

The rapport between Jesse and the detective deteriorated further as the day dragged on. While roaming the back alleys running parallel to the beach, they came across a crap game being played between separate clusters of trash cans. Cannon asked the player with the dice if he'd seen anyone matching Elkins' description. The player, a long-haired Latino with a diamond stud in his right earlobe, ignored Cannon and rolled the dice, winning a pot of several dollars. As he reached to fetch the money, however, the Latino had to pull his hand away to avoid having it stepped on by Cannon, who plopped one foot on the pot and squatted down until he was at the same eye level as the three youths caught up in the game.

Jesse managed to intervene and drag Cannon away before the situation grew out of hand, and the two men sparred verbally all the way to Venice Boardwalk, where Jesse wanted to question the proprietor of a weight-lifting gym club that Elkins supposedly had worked out at a few times. When the club owner refused to answer any questions, Cannon was quick to resort to strongarm tactics, only to be overcome by five of the club's musclebound members and escorted back out to the Boardwalk. Over the next few hours, Jesse and Cannon made ten other selective stops, each one producing no leads and each one straining relations to the point where it seemed that nothing short of a double homicide would keep the two men from taking out their frustrations on each other. As dusk approached, they decided to call it a day, having canvassed most of the Ocean Park-Venice area. There was one flyer left, however, and on a whim Jesse decided to leave it with one of his most trusted informers from his days as a street cop.

Bobby C. Corleone was a white, acne-scarred pimp who looked at the world through ochre-coloured glasses and wore a loud suit that looked as if it had been dipped in dayglo paint at a sixties revival. Jesse found him lording over his turf from behind the wheel of an old, perfectly-restored Oldsmobile Delta 88 that looked like a cross between a Cadillac and an airport limousine. As Jesse pulled into a parking spot next to the Olds, which was idling at a take-out burger joint, he told Cannon to roll down his window, then whistled to get Bobby's attention.

'Hey, if it ain't my man Mach!' Bobby drawled when he recognized Jesse. 'Been a while since I seen you and your hog in these parts. You get kicked upstairs or something?'

'That's right.' Jesse got out of his car and circled around to the Olds. He was only a few feet away from Cannon, and he lowered his voice as he slipped a twenty dollar bill from his wallet and handed it to Bobby, along with the flyer. 'Supper's on me, Bobby. I'm looking for somebody.'

Bobby quickly pocketed the twenty, then peeked at the picture of Elkins. 'Hey, check out that beard. Been trying to grow me just a goatee with no luck. What do you think his secret is?'

'You help me find him and I'll be sure to ask,' Jesse promised.

Bobby grinned and shifted his car into reverse. Two young women in tight hotpants and halter tops came out of the burger joint with several bags of fast food. 'You got any more of those twenties, Mach, and I can fix you and your partner up with some nice squeeze. See those ladies? They're mine. . . .'

'I don't want to know about it, Bobby, okay?' Jesse said. 'Just give me a call at the station if you spot that guy. *That* will be worth a couple more twenties to you. . . .'

Bobby tapped his studded ear. 'Loud and clear, my man.' As the two women got into his car, he added, 'You got to excuse me now, Mach. Me and the help need to fuel up before the night shift.'

Jesse backed away, letting Bobby pull out of his parking space and drive off.

'Oh, that's great,' Cannon grumbled from the Mustang. 'Here I thought you were going to try to come up with some consolation for this rotten day we've had, and the guy drives off with the goods. What gives?'

'Give it a rest, would you, Cannon?' Jesse got back in his car and reversed out into the street, then headed in the opposite direction as Bobby. 'Look, he's just a contact for information, not anything else as far as I'm concerned. You want to mix yourself up with prostitution, do it on your own time, after I drop you off. Where'd you say your hotel was?'

Cannon gave Jesse the name and address of the Ramada Inn he'd made reservations at during their lunch break, then lit up the last cigarette in his pack. 'Actually, though, I think that after a nice shave, a good shower, and a few stiff drinks, I'll be ready for more.'

'More what?' Jesse said as he drove.

'I say we keep on looking.'

'Frankly, Cannon, I don't give a damn what you say!' Jesse rolled down his window to let some fresh air creep into the Mustang and compete with the cigarette smoke. Glaring at Cannon out of the corner of his eye, he railed on, 'Thanks to your particular brand of bulldozer diplomacy, I'm the jerk who's had to pick up the pieces all day. You're out of your mind if you think I'm going to do it all night, too!'

'Touchy touchy,' Cannon sighed viciously. 'You're a wimp, Mach, that's your problem. When are you going to learn that you don't get anywhere playing soft with people, huh?'

'Not to change the subject or anything,' Jesse said, 'but exactly why is it you're so hot and bothered about getting your hands on Elkins, anyway? It's not like he's big league or anything. . . .'

'I told you back at the station, it's a matter of pride,' Cannon insisted. 'He got away from me . . . the first time that's ever happened. I aim to make sure it's the last time, too.'

'Well, it's going to have to wait until tomorrow.' Jesse pulled into the hotel and rolled to a stop alongside the front curb. 'For your sake and mine, let's hope we get him first thing in the morning. I'm sure you're anxious to get back to New York.'

Cannon grinned as he got out of the car. 'Probably not half as anxious as you are to see me go back, right?'

'Well, what do you know? For the first time all day you've said something I can agree with.' Jesse shifted his Mustang into first. 'I'll pick you up at around eight tomorrow. I'll have had breakfast already.'

'Good.' Cannon stood on the curb and watched Jesse drive off, then dropped his cigarette and crushed it under the heel of his Florsheims. 'You're lucky I need you to find Elkins, Mach . . .' he murmured under his breath.

The sun was down and the streets were bathed in the illumination of overhead lights. Instead of immediately checking into the hotel, Cannon walked down to the corner liquor store, where he purchased a pack of cigarettes and made sure he had a handful of spare change for a phone call. There was a telephone booth located in the store's parking lot. Cannon closed himself in it and dialled a number. Before the call could go through, an operator asked him to feed more money into the phone. Cannon complied, and as soon as he could hear the line ringing, he peered out, making sure there was no one watching him from the parking lot.

'Hello . . .' came the voice on the other end of the line. It was a deep, resonant voice, filled with quiet authority.

'Mr Girard. It's me, Cannon.'

'Hello, my friend. I assume you're calling from a public phone.'

‘Of course.’

‘Good. It’s my understanding that you’ve had a bit of bad luck. Is that correct?’

‘I’ll find him, don’t worry,’ Cannon promised. ‘I’ve never let you down before, have I?’

‘True enough. However, in this instance, I’m afraid there’s a second matter in addition to your earlier bungling.’

‘What are you talking about?’

‘The person you’re supposed to be . . . the *real* Detective Cannon . . . he’s been found. In the drainage ditch where you left him, I assume.’

Cannon kicked the base of the phone booth in anger. According to his original plan, he was to have gotten Girard’s money from Elkins and handed it over already. If things hadn’t gotten so fouled up, he’d have been on his way to a prolonged vacation in British Columbia instead of being stuck in Los Angeles, only a few miles from where his murder victim of the previous evening had been found. ‘I’ve got all his identification,’ he thought aloud, trying to look on some bright side to his current dilemma.

‘And they have his fingerprints,’ Girard reminded him.

‘It’ll take forty-eight hours before they get any positive make on him,’ Cannon said. ‘He’s just a John Doe until then.’

There was a moment’s silence on the other line, then: ‘Very well, you have a forty-eight hour reprieve. Don’t fail me, or there’ll be no place to hide from my wrath. But then I suppose you know that, don’t you?’

‘Yeah, I do,’ Cannon replied. ‘I’ll have your money, one way or another. I can’t guarantee I’ll be able to bring Elkins to you in one piece, though.’

‘Pity. If that’s to be the case, at least see to it that he dies slowly.’

‘You got it, Mr Girard.’ Cannon hung up the phone, then stepped out of the booth, opening his new pack of cigarettes as he stared out absently into the night and tried to think of his next move. He was already sure that he needed to act on his own, without Mach looking over his shoulder. That meant making a move now, tonight. But what . . .

'Of course!' he exclaimed to himself with sudden glee. There was one course that would produce his best chance of results, and he retreated back inside the phone booth to go for it. Dialling the police station, he had his call transferred to Communications, then reported, 'Hi, this is Detective Vincent Cannon. I'm on temporary assignment with Officer Jesse Mach. Are there any messages for us? We sent a lot of flyers around today. . . .'

ELEVEN

Norman Tuttle was a vitamin freak. Through the use of his computers, he had made careful calculations regarding the potency and release levels of various supplements and come up with a complicated schedule that required him to be popping pills of various sizes and shapes nearly every waking hour. Labelled dispensers were always close at hand at Street Hawk's command centre. Norman kept his bulk supplies in shelftop organizers normally used by weekend tinkerers to store nuts, bolts, and screws. As Jesse sat at the master control console that evening, he watched with wonder as Norman filled his palm with ten different capsules, pills, and tablets. Some were green, some white, and others housed in an amber gelatine coating.

'You're going to rattle when you walk if you down all those at the same time, Norman.'

Norman shook his head impatiently. 'Don't be silly, Mach. I don't plan to take them simultaneously. I spread them out, three every twenty minutes.'

'Oh, I see. That's much better.' Jesse snatched one of the capsules from Norman and held it up to the light. 'Any of these going to help you hit it off better with the ladies? I still can't believe you flubbed up at least four come-ons from that waitress this morning.'

'Give me that!' Norman took his capsule back and swallowed it with a couple others, then washed them down with a cup of bottled water. 'I'll have you know these are essential vitamins, taken in carefully prescribed dosages to ensure maximum efficiency. C . . . E . . . B1 . . . they augment my diet.'

'What ever happened to a nice simple balanced diet, Norman? I mean, maybe you should eat more . . . or at least eat better. What was that you had for brunch . . . pastrami on rye?'

'That's right . . . although from the looks of the bill you stuck me with, one might have thought I'd had filet mignon,' Norman complained. 'And let's get off the subject of waitresses, okay? Tell me some more about this new sidekick of yours . . . what's his name again?'

'Cannon. Vincent Cannon, New York's answer to Dirty Harry. And speaking of unpleasant topics, the less said about him, the better. Come on, let's hurry up and go over this new missile system you want to tack onto Street Hawk. I still have to call into the station before I crash. . . .'

'Then maybe you should call first,' Norman suggested, pointing to the phone as he rose from his seat and headed for the superbike, which rested on its custom-made pedestal in the holding area. 'It's going to take at least forty minutes to go over everything.'

'Forty minutes?' Jesse yawned as he dialled the station. 'Can't you just show me a diagram?'

'Sorry, it doesn't work that way.'

'Hello,' Jesse said into the phone when he got an answer. 'Communications? Right, this is Officer Mach. Any messages for me? . . . What!? I don't believe this! . . . Yeah, yeah, you better give it to me, too.'

Jesse grabbed a pen and scribbled down something on a scrap of paper, then thanked the communications officer and hung up, slamming the phone on its cradle.

'Trouble?' Norman asked him.

'Gee, how'd you guess? You take vitamins for deductive reasoning, too?'

'You don't have to take it out on me,' Norman said defensively.

'My "partner", the illustrious Detective Cannon, took one of my messages,' Jesse fumed. 'Fifteen minutes ago!'

'What message?'

'While I was making the rounds with Cannon, I slipped one of my contacts a twenty and told him to put out feelers on Elkins. He says he wants to meet, so he's probably got something for me . . . only five'll get you ten Cannon's on his way to pinch hit for me!'

Jesse stormed away from the console and headed for the lockers inside the exercise room. As he pulled out his Street Hawk suit, Norman moved over to the doorway and demanded, 'What do you think you're doing?'

'This guy Cannon is dangerous, in case you haven't gathered.' Jesse nearly ripped the buttons off his shirt in his haste to change. 'He would've killed Elkins if those guards hadn't stopped him. With all the people at the airport then, he would have picked off a fair share of innocent bystanders, too.'

'That's just speculation on your part,' Norman said. 'It seems to me that if this guy is a seasoned cop with high commendations, he wouldn't try something like that.'

'It's true, though,' Jesse insisted. 'I feel it.'

Norman sighed. It was the kind of condescending sigh used by university professors when dealing with misguided pupils. 'Conclusion without fact to back it up is no conclusion at all.'

'Oh, go take your vitamins, Norman,' Jesse said as he slipped into the racing outfit. 'Look, every time I don't listen to this intuition of mine, something bad happens. This time, I'm listening. . . .'

Norman tried to block the way when Jesse headed out of the exercise room, declaring, 'I can't justify the use of Street Hawk for—'

'Norman!' Jesse ploughed past his associate and headed for the bike. 'Trust me.'

'Where have I heard that before?'

As he straddled Street Hawk and slipped on his helmet, Jesse told Norman, 'We'll have to talk about that missile system later, okay?'

'Do I have a choice?'

'Not really. . . .'

Jesse propelled Street Hawk out through the parting billboard that served as the bike's gateway to the outside world, standing on his riding pegs and leaning slightly forward until the cycle was no longer airborne. According to the message he'd received from police communications, Bobby C. Corleone would be waiting in an alley behind the old Fairview Hotel on Bregmar Avenue at ten o'clock. It was already 9:57, and Jesse was well over a dozen miles from the rendezvous point, so he resorted to the usual combination of side streets and drainage channels to allow him to drive at speeds he wouldn't dare attempt in thicker traffic. Still, it took him over ten minutes to reach the Fairview and track down the alley in question.

Bobby was hunched over a milk crate, soaking a handkerchief in water dripping from a nearby spigot. His suit was torn and his face was discoloured by several bruises and lacerations. His blackened eyes were already puffing shut, but he squinted them even tighter when Street Hawk rolled into the alley and the bike's headlight washed over him.

'Hey, I had enough aggravation for one night!' he whined. 'Get outta my face with that beam!'

As he diverted the shaft of light to one side, Jesse called out, his voice distorted by the helmet, 'Was it Cannon?'

When he was able to make out the ominous figure on the bike, Bobby rose warily to his feet and took a step backwards, muttering, 'Who the hell wants to know? You from Mars or somethin' with that outfit? Get away from me!'

'Was it Cannon?' Jesse repeated. 'Answer me!'

Bobby backed into a trash can, startling himself. He dabbed at a cut on his lower lip with the wet handkerchief. 'Yeah, Cannon,' he divulged bitterly. 'Some cop named Cannon. Thinks he's Charles Bronson or something. . . .'

'What did you tell him?'

Overcoming his humiliation, the pimp sneered with a hint of his former bravado. 'Why should I tell you, huh? I mean, usually I get a little somethin' for my trouble when I—'

Jesse revved his engine and popped the clutch so that Street Hawk lunged slightly forward, its front wheel rising in the air. Bobby let out a frantic yelp and retreated behind the trash can. Jesse rode forward until he was only a few feet away.

'What did you tell Cannon?' Jesse demanded.

'Right, right!' Bobby said as he nervously crept out from cover. 'Cool it, okay? I told him Elkins is at a sleazebag dive off Grandview Boulevard. The Dunn House.'

'The Dunn House.'

'You got it . . . listen, do you know me or something?' Bobby wanted to know.

Jesse drowned out the pimp's voice with the roar of Street Hawk's engines. He only had a few feet of clear space to navigate between in the cluttered alley, but he continued speeding off, leaving Bobby far behind.

'You there, Norman?' he asked through his helmet microphone.

'Yes, I heard. I got a view of what that Cannon guy did to your contact's face. Maybe you were right about him, after all. I think we should hyper-thrust you over to Grandview Boulevard. . . .'

'I think you're right, Norman.'

TWELVE

Grandview Boulevard ran through the heart of Mar Vista, a small community situated a few miles inland from Venice and Ocean Park, Mitch Elkins' usual haunt. He'd taken a taxi to the Dunn House Hotel from the airport following his escape, then registered under an assumed name. His plan was to lay low and wait for the heat to blow over. Toward that end he'd spent nearly all his time the past twelve hours in his hotel room, venturing out only once for a quick bite of food at a burger joint down the block. He hadn't thought he'd run into anyone familiar, but an old acquaintance had spied him unwittingly while waiting in his car at the drive-through line, and it was that acquaintance who had later spilled the beans to Bobby C. Corleone while negotiating for the favours of one of the pimp's women. Now, at a little before ten-thirty, Elkins was in the midst of a run for provisions. He'd just loaded up on two sacks of miscellaneous groceries to tide him over in his room for a couple days. Beer and beef jerky were his primary staples, although he also made a feeble attempt to balance out his diet with some packaged cookies, a box of pretzels, and three cartons of Screaming Yellow Zonkers. For immediate consumption, he'd thrown in a quart of ice cream, and as he walked down the dim-lit sidewalk toward the Dunn House, condensation from the dessert container soaked through the bag, weakening it to the point where gravity could step in and lay claim to the groceries.

'Oh, this is just great!' Elkins complained as he bent down to retrieve his fallen food. To his left, he could see a pair of bedraggled transients huddled in the doorway of a closed shop, eyeing the groceries covetously. 'Either of you so much as touch this stuff and I'll grind your faces into that brick wall behind you, got it?!'

The homeless duo shrank back further into the shadows, saying nothing. Elkins went back to gathering up the runaway jerky and ice cream. He was faced toward approaching traffic, and when he happened to glance up at some of the passing cars, one particular face jumped out at him from across the intersection. Cannon was behind the wheel of a rental car, waiting for the light to change so he could turn onto Grandview.

'No. . . .'

Elkins wasn't sure if he'd been spotted yet, but he wasn't about to wait around and find out. Dropping his groceries back onto the sidewalk, the portly man began to pump his squat legs for all they were worth. It was the closest he could come to running, but nowhere near as effective. When the light at the intersection changed a few moments later, Cannon's car lunged forth and screeched as it took the corner sharply to take up the chase, ignoring the two tramps who had stole forth from the darkness to help themselves to Elkins' food and drink. Fortunately for Elkins, there was still enough traffic on Grandview to keep Cannon from catching up to him immediately. The squeal of tyres and blare of honking horns filled the fat man with increased fear, and he stared wildly ahead of him, looking for his best chance of escape. When he realized that there was an uninterrupted stretch of store fronts all the way to the corner, Elkins suddenly changed his course, backtracking to where he had passed a narrow passageway used for deliveries to the Dunn House Hotel.

Cannon had to slam on his brakes when Elkins started back toward the hotel. Two others cars came within inches of crashing into his rental sedan when he pulled an abrupt and flagrantly illegal U-turn in the middle of the boulevard. Ignoring the waving fists of the other motorists, Cannon spotted Elkins just as he was ducking into the alleyway and quickly followed in pursuit.

When Jesse sped onto the scene moments later, he startled the two transients, who had just succeeded in filling their pockets and arms with Elkins' involuntary donations. They both stared fearfully at the dark apparition before them, then hurried off into the night, spilling goods along the way.

Through his treated visor, Jesse quickly scanned the sidewalk and his attention was drawn immediately to the alleyway. From back at Street Hawk headquarters, Norman activated the visor's infra-red capabilities, providing Jesse with a clearer view of Cannon's car rolling into the narrow passageway. When the visor image was further enhanced, blowing up his view of the car, Jesse could make out the staggering figure of Mitch Elkins heading for the alley's dead end.

'There!' Norman's voice rang in Jesse's ear.

'I see. Let's hope I'm not too late. . . .'

Instead of heading directly for the alleyway, Jesse rode up onto the sidewalk and went down to the hotel's main driveway, which circled around to a parking lot behind the building.

Meanwhile, Elkins was just realizing the blunder he'd made, slowing down to face the eight foot high wooden barrier blocking his way. There were a few empty skids propped against the wall, and Elkins started to climb up them, hoping to reach the top of the wall and pull himself over. A shot suddenly thundered in the narrow confines, however, and when a bullet exploded through a wooden plank a foot away from Elkins' head, he froze in place and slowly looked over his shoulder.

Cannon left his engine running as he climbed out of his car and levelled his Magnum at Elkins, relishing the look of horror in the smaller man's eyes. 'We meet again, my friend,' Cannon said coldly. 'Perhaps we can get back to discussing our unfinished business now . . . something about some misplaced funds you were going to lead me to, I believe. . . .'

Elkins' throat was so tight and dry he could neither swallow nor speak. He could only throw his hands up in surrender and carefully climb down from the skids, nodding his head in hopes of conveying his intention of doing whatever it might take to keep that gun in Cannon's hand from firing again.

Cannon was about to pull back the hammer and order Elkins to talk when he became aware of a strange, mechanical howling sound coming from the other side of the fence. The noise became louder and closer, until it seemed as if something was about to crash through the wooden wall. Suddenly, the airborne silhouette of Street Hawk became visible in the glare of the sedan's headlights. The bike's vertical jets gave off trails of smoke like the breath of avenging dragons. Stunned by what he was seeing, Cannon dove quickly to one side and rolled across the asphalt as Jesse brought Street Hawk crashing down on the rooftop of the sedan, leaving an immense dent before he rode down the backside and landed with an artful skid on the pavement.

Cannon saw Elkins trying to take advantage of the distraction by scaling the wall once more, and he quickly raised his gun to shoot the fat man in the back. Before he could get the shot off, however, Street Hawk's .50 calibre machine guns strafed the walls of the alley above Cannon's head and along the side of his rental car, sending enough shrapnel flying to force Cannon to once more duck.

With extreme difficulty, Elkins heaved his bulk up against the fence and then pulled himself over, dropping down into the parking lot on the other side and rushing off in hopes of eluding capture once more.

Furious at the turn of events, Cannon scrambled to his feet and jumped inside his car, which hadn't been damaged to the point where he couldn't drive it. He shifted the vehicle into reverse, cutting the wheel sharply to one side so that he was coming at Street Hawk from an angle, eliminating the chances that Jesse could ride to one side and avoid a collision.

'Jesse, get out of the way!' Norman howled from across town, witnessing the approaching sedan through his monitors.

'No time,' Jesse said, dropping one foot to the gound and tilting his bike enough to lower the trajectory of his machine guns. When he unleashed another round of fire, the .50 callibre bullets obliterated the right rear tyre of Cannon's car, sending it out of control. Slamming into a stack of crates next to a concrete stairwell, the sedan firmly wedged itself in the alley, trapping Cannon.

'Dammit!' the man swore as he lurched out of the disabled auto. He'd jammed his shoulder and bruised his chest against the steering wheel from the force of the collision, and by the time he tracked down his fallen pistol and turned to take a shot at the man who had thwarted his attempt to nab Elkins, Jesse was riding out of the alley and turning the corner. One second he was in view; the next he was gone. . . .

THIRTEEN

When Jesse returned to Street Hawk Command Centre, he and Norman went over to the master control console and watched a taped replay of Jesse's arrival into the alley next to the Dunn House Hotel.

'As usual, instead of opting for the most prudent, and needless to say, less dangerous approach, you had to hop a fence and play demolition derby with a two ton sedan,' Norman griped as he watched the footage. 'If there had been a rack on the roof of that car, you would have been wiped out and I'd be there now with a broom and dustpan sweeping up your pieces.'

'If there had been a rack on the roof of that car, Norman, I wouldn't have landed the way I did,' Jesse defended himself. With a wicked grin, he added, 'I would have landed on the front hood instead. . . .'

On the monitor screen, both men stared at the replay of Cannon's last ditch attempt to pump bullets into Mitch Elkins' back. Because the footage had been taped from the perspective of Jesse's visor, the view was incredible and chilling in its dramatic composition. It was easy to look over Cannon's shoulder and see that the barrel of his gun was aiming at a spot directly between the fleeing man's shoulder-blades.

'He was going to waste that guy. No doubt about it,' Jesse said as he reached forward and froze the tape in midframe, leaving the monitor filled with the still image of the split second before the blasts from Street Hawk's machine guns had saved Elkins from certain death. 'But I still don't get it.'

'Get what?' Norman asked.

'Why? Why such a cold-blooded vendetta? I mean, it's not like Elkins is a big fish in anybody's pond.'

'Maybe Cannon wasn't actually going to kill him,' Norman speculated. 'Maybe he was just trying to goose Elkins with a little fear of the Lord, so to speak. . . .'

'I don't know. . . .'

'Think about it, Mach. There'd be two possibilities with that theory. On the one hand, rough as he is, Cannon might be a good enough cop to heed some professional ethics. He wasn't about to risk his badge killing Elkins, but Elkins had no way of knowing that. . . .'

Jesse made a face and shook his head as he started getting out of his racing uniform. 'That theory doesn't hold water with me, I'm afraid. What's the other angle?'

'On the other hand,' Norman said, 'Isn't it true that Elkins didn't have any payoff money on him when he was meeting the Kirksey brothers?'

Even before all of Norman's words were out of his mouth, Jesse's expression was changing from scepticism to exultation. He took a step forward and gave Norman a sharp slap on the back. 'Bingo! Cannon wants to lean on Elkins for the missing bucks. My God, it's so obvious, I can't believe I didn't figure it out myself. . . .'

As Norman rubbed his shoulder where Jesse had patted him, it was his turn to grin. 'Maybe you need to take some vitamins, Mach.'

On his way to the exercise room, Jesse licked his finger and scored the air. 'Point for Tuttle.' Once he had stripped down and stepped into the adjacent shower, he raised his voice so he could still carry on his conversation with Norman.

'No matter how you cut it, Cannon's a bad cop.'

'I'll buy that,' Norman shouted back as he went about cleaning Street Hawk. 'But I don't see that there's much you or I can do about it. If we blow the lid on him going after Elkins tonight, it would mean tipping our hat about Street Hawk, and that's out of the question.'

'Norman, there's nothing worth having a gun-happy cop on the street. Nothing. We have to do something.'

'You're right, of course.' Norman thought things over as he finished polishing Street Hawk and made a few minor adjustments to the power train and vertical lift mechanism. Once Jesse had finished his shower and had re-entered the exercise room to change back into his street clothes, Norman told him, 'Maybe it'd be a good idea if I slipped a computer query into the NYPD Personnel program. With any luck, I can get some background on Cannon . . . hopefully something we can tie in to what we know.'

'You can do that?'

Norman strode confidently back over to the command console and stroked one of the programming modules as if it were a prized pet. 'It might take me a while, but if it can be done at all, I'm the guy who can do it.'

'Oh, Norman, you're so diabolical. Why don't you flash some of that cockiness when you're around the ladies, hmm? You'd have 'em eating out of your hand.'

'You think so?' Norman said, genuinely interested. 'I mean, I thought women were turned off by intellectuals and technical jargon.'

'Naw, not a chance! This is almost the twenty-first century, pal! You can talk about nuclear physics on a hot date if you want to, as long as you can make it sound sexy.'

'Oh, come off it.'

'I'm serious, Norman.'

'I'll think about it.' Norman stared at his equipment as if in a new light. Before he could let himself get carried away on this new tangent, however, he forced his mind back to the matters at hand. Looking up at the still image on the playback monitor, he said, 'If the worst comes to the worst, we can always anonymously submit the tape of Cannon aiming at Elkins to the authorities.'

'Let's make that a last resort, Norman,' Jesse said, buttoning his shirt. 'In the meantime, try to get that background info. I'm going home and I'm going to try to catch some deep sleep. One way or another, I'm going to have to deal with Cannon, and I have this feeling I better be well-rested when I do. . . .'

FOURTEEN

Jesse arrived for work the following morning, buffered by eight hours of uninterrupted sleep. Cannon, however, had hardly slept at all, and it showed. The bogus detective was holding court in the middle of the squad room, venting his spleen and making a general nuisance of himself in the presence of Jesse's fellow officers.

'This creep on a motorcycle . . . this Street Hawk . . . who the hell is he, anyway?' Cannon demanded. 'What's he doing, flying around your town and interfering with police business?'

From his desk, Farnsworth called out, 'Why don't you tell us, New York? You seem to have all the answers.'

Cannon moved over to Farnsworth's desk and glowered down at the officer. 'I don't know what he's doing, but let me tell you something. If this was New York, we'd have him off the street . . . and probably six feet under!'

'In this town we don't snuff suspects before they've had a trial,' Jesse broke in, striding across the room to Cannon's side. 'And I want a word with you, detective.'

'Hollywood!' Cannon cracked a mocking grin at Jesse.

'Why so hot under the collar? Look, I'm sorry I didn't wait for you to pick me up, but I—'

'Don't peddle it on me, Cannon. I'm not buying.' Jesse pointed to the hallway. 'Let's step out.'

'Should I bring my gloves?'

Jesse let the retort slide past him. He turned his back on Cannon and strode past Rachel out of the squad room. Cannon followed close behind, but paused near Rachel and smiled. 'Changed your mind yet?'

'No,' Rachel replied, 'and I haven't lost it, either, so kindly buzz off . . . please.'

Cannon rolled his shoulders. 'Your loss, toots.'

Out in the hallway, Jesse wasted no time in getting to the point. Facing off with Cannon, he stated, 'I've got an informant. Name's Bobby C. Corleone. You met him with me yesterday, remember? Then you met him again last night and worked him over. You want to tell me why?'

'If you must know . . .' Cannon drawled slowly.

'Yes, I must. And it better be good.'

Cannon put his hands on his hips, refusing to look away from Jesse's stern gaze. 'The punk tried to swing on me when I wouldn't pay him,' he explained. 'He should have known better. Anybody with a brain in his head would have known better. . . .'

The implicit threat in Cannon's voice and words was not lost on Jesse, but he held his ground. 'When you got his message, why didn't you call me?'

Cannon took a step back and fished for his cigarettes. Once he had one lit, he spoke through the smoke. 'I don't need you to grab a wimp like Elkins.'

'Yeah? Well, that "wimp" got away from you, big man,' Jesse countered. 'Twice.'

Cannon had only taken a couple of puffs from his cigarette, but he dropped it on the linoleum and crushed it out as he flexed his fingers in and out of a fist. 'I'm a real religious guy, Mach,' he told Jesse. 'It says in the Bible, "Ask and ye shall receive", and it seems to me there's something you've been asking for since we first met. . . .'

Jesse dropped into a fighting crouch and was about to raise his fists in front of him when Altobelli came out into the hallway and bellowed, 'Cannon! Mach! Knock it off!'

The two combatants warily backed away from one another, letting the commander step between them.

'I just got a call from Uniformed Division,' Altobelli said. 'One of their boys thinks he just spotted Elkins.'

'Where?' Cannon asked.

'Washington and Lincoln, down in Venice. Nothing but a canal and alleys down there,' the commander explained for the out-of-towner's benefit. 'The area's been cordoned off and we're beginning to sweep through. I figured you two ought to be down there when they grab him.'

'Thanks, Commander,' Cannon said with mock sincerity. 'That was mighty white of you.'

Altobelli's recently dredged-up memories of Golden Glove matches were still on his mind, and he had no qualms about backing the larger man into the wall and sticking his jaw up so they could face each other eye-to-eye.

'Listen, hotshot. You want to pick a fight with anybody on this force, why don't you go straight to the top? I've been meaning to show the janitors the right way to mop a floor, anyway.'

Cannon's eyes pulsed with loathing, but he kept his mouth shut and squeezed away from Altobelli, then paced off down the hall. Jesse remained behind momentarily to trade a few words with his commander.

'I appreciate the thought, chief, but I don't need you to fight my battles for me. . . .'

'Let's not be selfish, Mach. That schmuck's got it coming from everyone in this entire department.'

'Yeah, I guess you're right.'

'Of course I'm right,' Altobelli maintained. 'Now go catch up with that idiot and keep an eye on him. I want Elkins in one piece.'

'If that was important to you, you shouldn't have bothered letting him know Elkins had been spotted, chief.'

'Better he should find out about it when you're with him, Mach. The more we keep him from acting behind people's backs, the more we'll be able to keep him in line and get him out of our hair.'

Jesse shook his head and started off, mumbling loud enough for Altobelli to hear, 'I hope I'm up for a medal when all this is over, because it sure qualifies for performance above and beyond the call of duty. . . .'

FIFTEEN

Norman had a sufficient security clearance to gain access to a wide range of highly sensitive computer information throughout the agency, but he rarely pulled his rank to secure such data. Behind his normally no-nonsense, stuffy exterior, a bit of a rogue lurked down deep in the corners of Norman's psyche, and he took joyful pride in his ability to surreptitiously tap into other computer banks. The better the safeguards against intrusion, the more he enjoyed the challenge. If he were ever to be tripped up in this admittedly clandestine practice, Norman always figured he could claim immunity on the basis of that time-honoured shield, that he was acting 'on top-secret orders paramount to matters of national security'. But he'd never been caught in the act before, and this morning was no exception. After several hours and more than two dozen programmed attempts, he finally succeeded in establishing contact with the New York Police Department's Personnel computer network. After he had put through a request for the information he was seeking, he had to wait less than a minute before his monitor screen came alive with background information regarding one Vincent A. Cannon, Detective First Grade.

As he scanned the data, Norman clucked his tongue with disappointment. According to the computer records, Cannon was an exemplary cop with commendations galore and no skeletons in his closet.

'Drat,' he whispered, turning from the screen momentarily to fill his palm with his latest dose of vitamin supplements. After swallowing the pills, he sipped down what was left in his glass of mineral water and almost spat it back out when he looked back at the screen. Through the miracle of computer graphics, a picture of Detective Cannon was materializing before Norman's eyes. This man was thin-faced, bespectacled, and had a receding hairline. He in no way bore any resemblance to the man Norman had seen preparing to blow away Mitch Elkins in the alley next to the Dunn House Hotel the night before.

'I don't believe it!'

Norman shut off the computer and rushed to his phone, putting a quick call through to the police station. When there was an answer on the other line, he blurted out, 'I need to speak to Officer Jesse Mach in Public Relations . . . quickly, please. This is an emergency!'

The woman dispatcher put Norman on hold momentarily, then replied, 'I'm sorry, but he's in the field right now. Can I take a message?'

'Yes. It's imperative that you get a message to him,' Norman insisted. 'I guarantee you, it's a matter of life and death. . . .'

When Jesse and Cannon arrived in Venice, the area was aswarm with other police vehicles and uniformed officers laying out a dragnet. Civilian traffic was being turned away from all streets running parallel to the murky canals, and suspicious vehicles were being searched before being allowed to leave the vicinity. Teams of officers were checking under the high-arched bridges that spanned the waterways, while others prowled the shrub-choked embankments and adjacent neighbourhoods, on the alert for Mitch Elkins, who was reportedly armed and dangerous now, having taken a few shots at the patrolmen who had originally spotted him in the area.

'Looks like half the force is as antsy about getting Elkins as you are, Cannon,' Jesse remarked as they headed over to confer with the supervising officer on the scene, Lieutenant Peter Pereinal, a handsome black man who was also the toughest centre in the police basketball league.

Cannon seemed to have mixed emotions about the dragnet, and he eyed the other officers dourly as he muttered, 'We could save the taxpayers a lot of money if they'd just let me get Elkins on my own.'

'It's not like you didn't have your chance,' Jesse reminded the man.

Lieutenant Pereinal was running things from the back end of his station wagon, referring to an area map laid out on the tailgate and barking occasionally into either his walkie-talkie or a portable radio microphone. When he glanced up and spotted Jesse, he said, ''lo, Mach. How's the knee?'

'I can get around,' Jesse said, 'but it's going to be a while before I start shooting hoops again.'

'Too bad. We miss you on the back court.'

Jesse introduced Pereinal to Cannon, who gruffly asked, 'What's the latest on Elkins?'

'Still at large,' the lieutenant said. 'People aren't being much help, either. Four people say they've seen him heading south, toward the airport. Another couple claim he hopped a cab heading up to Santa Monica. We're fanning out right now. You want to join in? We could use some help up around the pier. . . .'

'Sure thing,' Jesse said.

'Wait a second,' Cannon said. 'Is that the Santa Monica Pier you're talking about?'

'Yeah,' Pereinal answered. 'What about it?'

'My guess is he's gone the other way, toward the airport.'

'Well, I've got that area covered,' the lieutenant said with a touch of anger. 'If you want to help, check the pier, okay?'

Cannon looked like he was ready to dispute the assignment, but Jesse cut in, saying, 'We're on our way. Come on, detective. . . .'

Cannon badmouthed the lieutenant all the way back to Jesse's Mustang, and when he kept it up while they were driving down Third Street toward Santa Monica, Jesse tuned him out rather than get himself involved in yet another argument. As they were driving past Rose Street, Jesse pulled over, recognizing the old woman from Elkins' former apartment. She was standing with a group of children near a parked squad car, talking with a pair of uniformed officers. When he got out of the car, the woman recognized him and waved.

'Officer Mach! I was just telling this man I knew you!'

As Cannon grudgingly joined him, Mach conferred with the other officers, one of whom was Farnsworth, who said, 'She and a couple of the kids say Elkins slipped into her room while she was down checking for her mail. When she tried to confront him, he ran for it.'

'Which way?' Cannon asked.

Farnsworth pointed. 'Toward the beach. We've already called it in, so . . .'

Cannon turned heel and headed back for the Mustang, telling Mach, 'Let's hit it!'

Before obliging Cannon, Jesse grinned at Farnsworth. 'The guy's got real charm, know what I mean?'

'Yeah, right. Why don't you take him to the end of the pier and tell him to take a jump.'

'I might just do that.' When Jesse returned to his car, Cannon was already inside, fiddling with the police radio. 'What's the matter? Did I just get a call?'

Cannon shook his head. 'Just an APB update on Elkins. Let's go!'

'I'm going already!'

They drove in silence the rest of the way down Third Street to Santa Monica, then turned left on Pico Boulevard, which linked them up with Ocean Avenue and then the strip of roadway running down the pier. In its prime half a century before, the Santa Monica Pier had been a glitzy, tourist-packed haven, complete with roller coaster and rows of shops and arcades. Now, however, the coaster was only a memory, and a few fierce storms had launched powerful waves that had torn down large sections of the decaying pier, which had already become but a dreary shadow of its former glory. Most of the shops were gone or boarded up, and tourist traffic was thin . . . and even thinner this morning, now that a police barricade had been set up at the entrance to the pier.

Aside from the officers tending to the barricade, Jesse and Cannon were the first authorities on the scene, and as they began to search the establishments lining either side of the roadway, they took turns asking if anyone had seen Elkins in the area. Nobody had.

'Dammit!' Cannon cursed, kicking the wooden slats of the boardwalk. 'Where is he?'

'I'm going to ask that guy running the bumper car ride,' Jesse said. 'Why don't you check at that hot dog stand across the way?'

The two men split up, and as he approached the stand, Cannon turned to look in the direction of a low-flying police helicopter that was banking close over the pier's old, boarded-up merry-go-round, which had been used over the years as a backdrop for many a motion picture. The chopper soon pulled away from the structure and floated along the coastline, but Cannon's attention remained fixed on the merry-go-round, where he thought he had seen signs of movement in the gap between some of the windows. Cannon quickly shot a glance Jesse's way, making sure the other man was preoccupied with questioning the bumper car operator, then picked up his stride and hurried toward the merry-go-round. He circled to the back of the building, where he found the door to the employee's entrance was slightly ajar. Closer observation revealed that the door's lock had been tampered with.

'Yes . . .' Cannon murmured under his breath as he pulled out his service revolver and entered the dark enclosure. He lingered just inside the doorway for several seconds, letting his eyes accustom themselves to the drastic change in light. Only a few stray beams of sunlight poured into the merry-go-round, but eventually the interior took on shape and he could make out the outline of mounted horses on the idle carousel and the upright pipes of a vintage steam organ. Across the room, there was a ticket booth and a popcorn machine. A figure was lurking between the two objects, his back turned to Cannon. When he took a step forward, Cannon's shoes pressed against a loose floorboard.

Mitch Elkins whirled around to find himself staring down the business end of Cannon's revolver. He had a gun of his own, but it was out of bullets and, taken by surprise, he didn't think fast enough to try bluffing.

'Hold it, Elkins, or you're dead,' Cannon called out.

As the man with the gun moved toward him, Elkins slowly held his hands out at his sides, holding his own gun flatly in his palm to indicate that he had no plans to use it. 'If you kill me, you'll never know where the money is. You'll—'

'I already told you the money's got nothing to do with me, Elkins.'

'Maybe it should,' Elkins suggested.

Cannon took a few steps forward and grabbed Elkins' gun. 'Why's that?'

'What's Girard paying you for this job?' Elkins bartered.

Cannon raised an eyebrow. 'Why do you ask? You got something particular in mind?'

'A deal,' Elkins proposed. His throat was dry and he had to swallow a few times before he could go on talking, all the while gazing at the gun pointed at his chest. 'We can work it out. You can have seventy-five per cent. I just need enough to get out of the country and set something up . . . I'm talking a lot of money!'

'Seventy-five per cent?' Cannon said the words as if they were unpleasant additions to his vocabulary.

'All of it!' Elkins gasped when he saw the hammer being drawn back on Cannon's revolver. 'You can have it all. Just give me ten grand and let me go . . . don't kill me, please!'

Cannon stared hard at the bearded man, then slowly lowered his gun. 'I'm in a good mood today,' he said with a tight smile. 'I tell you what. You convince me your offer's on the level and I'll let you keep fifty. . . .'

*

Walking away from the bumper car ride, Jesse looked around for Cannon. Not seeing the man, he was at once alarmed and angry with himself for having taken his eyes off the detective.

'Cannon!' he shouted, pacing down the pier and looking from side to side. 'Hey, Cannon, where are you!'

He was about to question the cook at the hot dog stand when a gunshot echoed out from inside the merry-go-round building. Jesse whipped out his pistol and hurried toward the direction of the outburst, already fearing the worst. Other officers were already on their way as well. He didn't bother circling around to the back of the building. Reaching the front doorway, he paused a moment, then leaned his full weight into one of the wooden panels blocking the window. The panel gave way and clattered to the floor and Jesse tumbled into the bleak chamber, holding his gun out in front of him.

'No. . . .'

Mitch Elkins was lying face down on the carousel between two sculpted horses. Cannon was nowhere to be seen.

SIXTEEN

Jesse was back in his car, returning to the police station, when the dispatcher was finally able to get through to him with Norman's urgent message about Cannon being an imposter.

'It's a little late, but thanks,' Jesse said before snapping off the police radio. He banged his fist against the dashboard in frustration. Of all the days for him to forget to wear the beeper that linked him with Norman's command centre. If only he'd remembered it. If only he'd been in the car the handful of other times the dispatcher had tried to reach him prior to their arrival at the pier. 'If . . . if . . .'

Cannon was still on the loose, although the dragnet that had been cast for Elkins was now concentrating on the search for his killer. The more he thought about it, the more Jesse began to realize that perhaps it was fortunate the dispatcher hadn't gotten through to him earlier. If the message had been relayed while Cannon was in the car with him, it seemed likely to Jesse that he would have found himself an immediate target for the imposter's revolver. It was a small consolation, however, and when he pulled into the station, Jesse's mood was still sour. Once inside, he put a quick call through to Norman to assure him that he was okay but that Cannon had escaped after killing Elkins.

'So much for my "conclusion without fact is no conclusion at all",' Norman said. 'You were right all the time, Mach. . . .'

'*That* fact doesn't make me feel any better, Norman.'

'What are you going to do now?'

'I'm not really sure. Altobelli's requested a telephonic dupe of Cannon's file from New York. It should be coming in any time now, and that will officially point out that we're dealing with an imposter without us having to tip your hand.' Glancing up from his desk, Jesse saw Rachel entering the squad room. He told Norman, 'I'll keep you posted. I gotta go now. Thanks for the concern.'

'I just wish I could have been quicker in tapping into the computers in New York,' Norman said. 'I mean, if I hadn't played around trying to be Super Hacker, I might have been able to—'

'It's not your fault, Norman,' Jesse interrupted. 'Give yourself a break. I'll see you soon.'

'Yeah. Stay safe, Jess.'

Jesse hung up slowly, touched by Norman's rare display of humility and concern. So maybe there lurked some real emotions behind that intellectual barrier the engineer so often surrounded himself with.

'Still nothing yet on Cannon,' Rachel informed Jesse as she strode up to the desk.

'That's not his name.'

'I know,' she said, 'but we have to call him something.'

'I have some ideas, but they aren't names to be tossed about in polite company.' Jesse shook his head miserably. 'I can't believe he was able to walk around here making life miserable for everyone . . . and he wasn't even a cop! God, he must have been gloating inside at pulling that off.'

'Well, at least I'm glad I had the good sense to say no when he put the make on me,' Rachel sighed. 'I'd hate to think what his idea of a date might be.'

The two of them stewed in their collective funk for a while longer, but when an officer rushed into the squad room with a manila file and made a beeline for Altobelli's office, Jesse said, 'I think the lowdown on our man's just arrived.'

As if to confirm Jesse's suspicions, Altobelli leaned out of the doorway of his cubicle and snapped at Jesse and Rachel, 'Hey, you two! Get in here, on the double!'

As they headed for the commander's office, Rachel told Jesse, 'You ought to take up palm-reading in your spare time, you know?'

'Sounds pretty good right now,' Jesse responded, holding the door open for Rachel, then closing it once they were both in the office. On Altobelli's desk, they could both see the official photos of the real Vincent A. Cannon. The commander tapped a pencil on top of the other information in the file that had been brought to him.

'Sorry I didn't listen to that intuition of yours, Mach,' he apologized. 'But I didn't, and that's the end of the hair-tearing. We've got a killer out there and I want him. I want him bad.'

'Me, too, chief,' Jesse said. 'No luck with the dragnet?'

Altobelli shook his head. 'He had a few minutes before word got out that we should be looking for him instead of Elkins. That's plenty of time for somebody who wants to make himself scarce.'

'Airports, bus stations, trains,' Rachel brainstormed aloud.

'Way ahead of you,' Altobelli said, going to the one wall in his office that had a window facing the streets. 'If he didn't get out in the first hour after the shooting, then he's out here somewhere. . . .'

'I don't think he got out, chief,' Jesse speculated. 'I think he had something to pick up first.'

'Another feeling?' Rachel asked.

'No,' Jesse said with a stiff grin. 'This time, I've got more to go on. There's an ace up our sleeves that we've been forgetting about.'

'What's that?' Altobelli asked.

'Not what,' Jesse corrected. '*Who* . . .'

SEVENTEEN

The Kirksey brothers weren't big fans of life behind bars, and it showed. Wearing prison fatigues instead of their customary flashy suits, they looked somehow smaller and less powerful, although the dour expression on their faces suggested that strong emotions were smouldering behind their ruthless eyes. They were sitting on bunks in their prison cell, arms crossed in front of them, doing their best not to cooperate with Jesse, who was on his feet between them, waiting for results. From the impatient look on his face, it was clear that he wasn't getting much.

'Jail, you understand,' Al said with a deliberately annoying lilt to his voice, 'is not our favourite place.' He'd been spouting variations on this same mantra ever since Jesse had shown up. Jesse knew that Al was trying to strike a deal in exchange for talking, but he wasn't about to give in to the older brother's underhanded lobbying.

'I couldn't care less what you think about being in jail,' Jesse told both prisoners. 'You had plenty of time to think about that before you went on this robbery and burglary spree of yours. You hit four places in as many weeks. And you hit 'em armed. . . .'

'We never killed anyone!' Tommy spouted defiantly.

Al stared daggers at his kid brother and told him, 'Shut up, Tommy.'

'Well, it's true!'

'It's beside the point is what it is,' Jesse retorted. He looked over his shoulder at the two officers standing outside the cell door, half-heartedly keeping an eye on the men inside. One of the officers grinned at Jesse and patted the handle of his nightstick.

'Hey, Mach, if you want to get them to talk, just let me and my little friend have a word with 'em.'

'Thanks, but you'd probably only break your stick over the rocks in their heads,' Jesse cracked. He turned back to the brothers. 'You showed up at that factory with the jewels. Elkins met you and said he didn't have the money, but he started to tell you where he was keeping it when the cops showed up.'

'Guess again,' Al said. 'It wasn't the cops that broke things up at first—'

'Yeah, it was that Evil Knievel dude on the superbike,' Tommy said. 'Man, that was sure one crazy set of wheels he had!'

'Let's forget about that part, okay?' Jesse said. 'How much did Elkins tell you about the location of the money?'

Tommy snorted bitterly, 'Sure as hell not enough that we could – yeooww!!'

Al's right toe lashed out and caught his younger brother squarely on the shin, shutting him up. Tommy rubbed the spot where he'd been struck and glared at his brother, but said nothing. Al looked up at Jesse and claimed, 'I don't know what you're talking about, officer. What's more, I want to see my lawyer. Right now.'

'Al . . .'

'Hey, I got rights, copper!'

'Maybe so, but you don't have enough info on that money to get to it after you've done your time,' Jesse bluffed. 'Think about it. You're stonewalling me on a lost cause.'

Al went back to his standard response. 'It's all these bars, officer. Something about bein' stuck in jail just messes my mind up terrible. I forget all kinds of things, if you know what I mean. . . .'

Jesse was pretty sure he wasn't going to get any answers without bargaining with the prisoners. Much as he was against cutting deals he began to negotiate.

'You lost the ace, Al. Why not settle for a couple deuces?'

Al narrowed his eyes and mulled over the proposition, trying to read between the lines and figure out what Jesse was offering. He finally guessed, 'You can drop the sentence by four years?'

'Do I look like a judge?' Jesse saw a gleam of hunger come to Al and Tommy's eyes. He had them. 'I can suggest two. But I want to know what Elkins told you first, dammit, and I want to know now!'

'Hey, back off, man. I need room to think!' Al said, waving Jesse away from him.

Tommy didn't need room to think. The thought of having his sentence reduced was all he needed to know. He stood up and told Jesse, 'Can't we do somethin' like be State witnesses? You know, give you the stuff and we go free?'

'Tommy, sit down and shut up!' Al barked, grabbing his brother by the shirt-tail and pulling him back onto his bunk. 'I do the talking for us around here.'

'Well, you damn well better make up your minds,' Jesse said, glancing down at his watch. 'If I walk out of here without the information I'm looking for, you're out of luck, period. This is your last chance!'

'Wait a minute!' Tommy sputtered. He turned to Al, his eyes wide with desperation. 'Come on, bro! We got a shot at some light time here! Man, I don't want to rot up in the State pen!'

'Shut up, Tommy!' Al rose from his bunk and turned his back to Jesse, pacing slightly in the cramped confines of the cell, lost in thought. When he finally reached a decision, he returned to his cot and sat back down, reaching to his shirt pocket for his cigarettes. 'Okay,' he told Jesse. 'I'll talk. . . .'

EIGHTEEN

'This reminds me of *Citizen Kane*,' Norman said as he punched out a program on his computer.

'How's that?' Jesse asked. He'd come to the command centre immediately after talking to the Kirksey brothers.

'Don't tell me you've never seen that movie,' Norman groaned. 'I mean, culturally deprived as you are, I would have at least thought that at some point in your life you might have—'

'Norman, I saw the movie,' Jesse told him. 'I just don't get the connection.'

'Remember how Charles Foster Kane's last words were "Rosebud"? And how practically the whole movie dealt with trying to figure out what he meant?'

'Okay, now I see what you're getting at,' Jesse said as he saw Norman typing three words into the computer. 'Only in our case, instead of "rosebud", we have a wider selection.'

'Bravo,' Norman cheered sarcastically. 'Okay, we have "monarch", "demo", and "Garland Boulevard". That's it, right?'

'Yeah.' Jesse nodded, taking a step back from the command module. 'And I quote Al Kirksey himself . . .

"Elkins only managed to get a couple of words out before that space cadet arrived and screwed things up." '

'Space cadet, huh?' Norman glanced up at his monitor screens, waiting for his programmed request to be answered by the computers. 'He certainly has a way with the English language, doesn't he?'

'Compared to his brother, the man's almost eloquent.'

One of the monitor screens flashed with a Los Angeles map depicting the area bi-sected by Garland Boulevard. The other screen began filling up with a cross-referenced listing of people and streets named Monarch. In the case of people or businesses located on Garland Boulevard or Streets called Monarch that intersected with Garland, the names were underscored.

'Once we've culled through any leads this turns up,' Norman explained, 'I'll tap into newspaper files for any news on demonstrations, demo tapes, or demolitions and see if that gets us anywhere.'

'You know, Norman, if they had had this kind of technology forty years ago, *Citizen Kane* might have ended up being a very short movie. That one reporter would have just punched "rosebud" into a computer and—'

'Aha!' Norman shouted, pointing at the screens. 'Bingo! Take a look there on the left. There's a Monarch Theatre on Garland Boulevard.'

'All right. . . .'

Norman made a note of the address and enhanced the map image on the screen, blowing it up to include all the area within a one-block radius of the Monarch Theatre.

'You know, there's something about this that sounds familiar,' Norman said. 'I could swear I remember reading or hearing something about the Monarch in the past few weeks. Do you?'

Jesse shook his head as he went over to the phone. 'Let me have their number for programme information. Maybe that will give us a clue.'

Norman called out the number, then started typing out a new program, this time asking his computers to skim through all the local papers for headlines featuring the

Monarch and any reference to demonstrations or demolitions.

'There's just a taped message,' Jesse told Norman as he hung the phone up. 'The number's out of service and there's no new number.'

'I know why,' Norman said as he spotted the first news item to flash up on the screen, taken from a recent issue of the *Los Angeles Times*. 'The theatre's been closed for months. And get this . . . it's because they plan to demolish that whole block of Garland to make way for a shopping plaza!'

'When?'

They both skimmed through the article for mention of a date. Norman spotted it first. 'The third . . . that's—'

'—today!' Jesse finished the sentence as he turned from the command module and headed for his locker in the exercise room. 'They must have a demolition crew crawling all over the place down there. With any luck, they've kept Cannon away, or at least they might remember having seen him.'

When Norman saw Jesse starting to change into his Street Hawk riding suit, he protested, 'Let the police take care of this, Mach.'

'I *am* the police, remember?' Jesse quickly climbed out of his street clothes and stepped into the snug-fitting riding pants. 'Besides, I'm the one who let Cannon get to Elkins. This one's between him and me.'

'Be serious, Mach! Look, the odds are that the demolition's already taken place, anyway. Why risk any unnecessary exposure on the bike?'

'The article said the charges wouldn't go off until after three.' Jesse checked his watch. 'I've still got close to an hour. I'll be discreet getting there.'

Norman watched dubiously as Jesse paced across the room in his racing suit and climbed onto Street Hawk. 'On that bike and in that uniform, you're going to be as discreet as a clown at a funeral, Mach!'

Jesse wasn't about to be deterred, however. He slipped on his helmet, then asked Norman, 'Did you fuel this baby up for me?'

'I always fill the tank after you've been on a run. You know that.'

'Well, I'm off, then. Wish me luck, Norman.'

Norman ran his hand through his hair and let out a sigh of exasperation. 'When will I ever learn that I can't help you out without you thinking you have *carte blanche* use of Street Hawk?'

'Probably never,' Jesse told him. 'Unless, of course, there's some vitamins you can take for it.'

Norman was going to respond to Jesse's friendly jibe, but he was drowned out by the sound of Street Hawk's motor warming up for another run on the town. Instead, he mumbled under his breath, 'What's the use. . . .'

NINETEEN

The block on Garland Boulevard that housed the Monarch Theatre had been barricaded even more securely than the Venice area during the morning search for Mitch Elkins. No one at all was allowed inside the boundary staked out by rows of yellow sawhorses. Bright signs were posted on each of the barriers, explaining that the block was being closed off due to the pending use of heavy explosives. Of course, the prospect of seeing an entire city block demolished in one carefully-executed series of dynamite blasts was too much for many people to overlook. Media helicopters were hovering high above the targeted sight, and an entrepreneur a quarter mile away was selling tickets to curiosity seekers who wanted to watch the demolition from atop his four-storey parking structure. Other spectators were gathered at the windows of nearby skyscrapers, peering through binoculars and periodically checking their clocks. The official time of the detonation was 3:05, a mere four minutes away.

The Monarch Theatre was an old movie house, one of the last opulent structures to go up during the mid-forties, when such construction was reaching its peak. Regrettably, the theatre had not aged well over the years, due to a combination of poor location and mediocre management. For a period in the late sixties, the Monarch had experienced a brief rush of business when it had been turned into a porno theatre, but when neighbourhood pressure had pushed those owners out of the area, the once-regal structure had begun to slowly deteriorate, in direct proportion to the flagging attendance at its second and third-run feature presentations. Token efforts had been made to save the structure from destruction, but now the demolition crew was hard at work preparing the final touches that would ensure the Monarch's consignment to memory.

Two hard-hatted workers slowly backed out of the main entrance, paying out wire from a large wooden reel. The doors to the Monarch had been removed, and the wire led in through the lobby and branched out to the various explosive charges that had been strategically placed at points that would provide the surest undermining of the foundation when they were detonated.

When they reached their Jeep, parked in front of the theatre, the men carefully hoisted the reel and set it into a bracket that would allow it to feed out more wire as the vehicle was moving. One man climbed in the back to watch over the reel while his partner took the driver's seat and slowly pulled away.

Vincent Cannon was crouched in the shadows across from the Monarch, and he remained in hiding as he watched the Jeep head down the block, trailing wire behind it. Halfway down the block, the Jeep pulled to a stop behind a specially constructed demolition terminal. The crew superintendent, a beefy man whose jaws were clamped around an unlit cigar, snipped the wire on the Jeep's reel, then handed it over to a colleague, who fastened the end to one of eighteen separate relay detonator switches.

'Okay, that's it!' the super called out to his men. 'Tell our choppers to make one more pass and let's go once around the block with a bullhorn to make sure no one's in there . . . then we'll be ready for showtime!'

The crew members let out expectant cheers as they went

about their final preparations. As the Jeep backed away from the terminal, then headed off down the block so the last warnings could be given, Cannon withdrew further into the shadows across from the Monarch.

'Everyone please evacuate the area!' the man in the Jeep called out through his battery-powered megaphone. 'We'll be setting off the explosives in less than three minutes! Please evacuate the area!'

Once the Jeep had passed, Cannon crept forth from his cover and looked both ways down Garland Boulevard to make sure no one was watching, then he bolted across the street. Just as he was reaching the curb, he was startled by the whirring of a low-flying helicopter coming towards him from between two large buildings. Throwing himself to the ground, he crawled on all fours until he was able to hide beneath a bench at the bus stop in front of the theatre. When the helicopter seemed to be hovering in position directly overhead, Cannon carefully pulled out his revolver and undid the safety.

Jesse was nine blocks away, sticking to side streets as he usually did when travelling in the daytime. Norman was keeping track of his position and giving him directions through Jesse's helmet speakers.

'I hate to bring this up so late in the ballgame, Mach, but I hope you realize that the area's apt to be cordoned off and heavily guarded. How do you propose to get past them without being stopped . . . or, worse yet, identified as Street Hawk and put under arrest?'

'I'm sure I'll think of something,' Jesse assured his partner. 'Now, do I take a turn up here?'

'Yes, a right. And can't you be more specific?'

'What, about what I'm going to do?' Jesse said. 'You know, Norman, that's where you and I differ. I like to leave a little room open for spontaneity, improvisation. You should really try it sometime.'

'Maybe I will, but when I do, it won't be with a multi-million dollar motorcycle, you can be sure of that!'

★

The helicopter belonged to one of the local television stations, and it had moved into a holding pattern above the theatre in hopes of getting the most dramatic shots of the demolition. A second chopper soon drifted close by, and word was passed along that the news team was flying too close to the buildings and would have to pull back at least a few hundred yards. Even with a bullhorn being used to convey the message, Cannon was barely able to hear any of the words above the drone of the two 'copters, and he almost broke from his cover prematurely, fearing that he'd been spotted for sure and was going to be apprehended. A few extra seconds of patience paid off for him, however, and soon the two aircraft flew off.

Cannon rolled out from under the bench and hurriedly dashed inside the theatre. Before shooting Elkins, he'd managed to learn that the missing money had been stuffed into one of the dummies stored in the backstage area of the theatre, which was owned by an acquaintance of Elkins who had briefly entertained the notion of putting on stage plays before he had sold out the Monarch to the firm that was going to put up the shopping plaza. As he stepped over the detonation wire and passed through the lobby into the theatre itself, Cannnon had to stifle a sneeze stirred up by the loose dust floating in the stagnant air. The odour of decay assailed his nostrils as well. It was the smell of mildew and wood rot, reminding him of the boathouse where he had killed the man whose name he had been using the past few days. A strange eeriness crept over him as well when he moved down the main aisle of the deserted interior, approaching the sagging velvet curtain that stretched the length of the stage. The movie screen had already been removed, sold on the side by the owner several weeks before. When he reached the stage, Cannon turned around and pulled out his gun. All the chairs in the theatre were empty, and there was no one visible behind the small windows of the projection booth in the balcony, but he still sensed a presence in the theatre besides his own. He finally shook off the feeling, however, and climbed up the steps leading to the stage, then moved behind the curtains, shaking loose more dust and almost triggering another sneezing attack.

There was a divider directly behind the curtains, and Cannon had to grope in relative darkness to find the door that had been built into it. When he pushed the door open and stepped into the backstage area, Cannon suddenly froze and whipped his gun into firing position. He almost had squeezed off a shot when he realized what he was seeing and relaxed.

Before him, stacked in haphazard disarray, were nearly a dozen old manikins and a variety of other junk that was beyond salvaging. Sets of lifeless eyes stared at Cannon, triggering the anger that had come over him once he'd shaken off his fear.

'Damn you, Elkins!' he spat contemptuously. The money could be in any one of the dummies, and Elkins hadn't bothered to mention which one, much less the fact that there were so many of them. Cannon strode across the creaking flooboards and slammed the head of the closest manikin with the butt of his pistol. The head toppled off, revealing nothing. Before he moved on to the next dummy, Cannon first sidetracked to the controls that operated the curtains, opening them wide enough to let a little more light filter into the backstage area. Then he returned to the manikins and ripped off the head of one of them with his bare hands. Still no money.

Jesse was now nearing the barricades that surrounded the detonation area, and he began circling around the block, trying to remain inconspicuous at the same time as trying to find a way past the obstacles. Norman was buzzing apprehensively in his ear, 'This is crazy! There's no way you can get in!'

'Calm down, Norman,' Jesse said. 'When I was a kid I used to sneak into theatres all the time. They never caught me.'

'This is hardly the same thing, Mach!'

'We'll see about that. I still have a little time left. . . .'

★

'Two minutes and forty-five seconds!' the foreman shouted before jamming his cigar back in his mouth. He was standing near the detonation terminal, conferring with his underlings by way of walkie-talkie. His assistant was double-checking the connections on all eighteen of the terminal switches.

'I think we're all set here, sir,' he reported to his boss.

'Good.' Once he had stepped behind the walls of the sub-station, the superintendent pulled a lighter from his pocket and flicked a flame into life. 'Start the countdown at two minutes,' he declared before applying the fire to his cigar.

Cannon had dismembered half the manikins, succeeding only in adding more fuel to his growing rage. After checking his watch, he called Elkins a few names that would have made a sailor blush, then tore into the next dummy with psychopathic fury. When the manikin's torso cracked open, a shower of twenty-dollar bills tumbled forth.

'Yes!' Cannon exulted, throwing the figurine to the floor and ripping the torso wide open so that he could get at all the money stored within. From the looks of it, there were thousands, maybe hundreds of thousands of dollars there for the taking. With almost manic glee, Cannon began cramming wads of the currency into his pockets, chortling to himself at his seeming triumph.

The festivities were short-lived, however, because the whine of a high-performance engine soon directed Cannon's attention to the back of the theatre, where he was startled to see the silhouette of Street Hawk, lit from behind by the unblocked entrance to the lobby.

'No you don't!' Cannon seethed, scrambling away from the manikin to where he had set down his gun earlier. 'Nobody stops me now!'

'One minute to detonation!' Norman was pleading in Jesse's ear. 'Get out of there!'

'I just got here, Norman,' Jesse said before popping the clutch and veering his bike sharply to one side, avoiding the gunshot that ripped into the doorframe behind him. He manoeuvred Street Hawk along the back row of seats, leaning the bike to one side to make a smaller target of himself. Cannon was blowing holes in several of the seats with his gun, getting closer to his intended mark with each shot.

'Jesse, you aren't bulletproof!' Norman pleaded. 'If you have to, just take him out with the particle beam and leave!'

'I want him alive,' Jesse declared, ducking still another shot. He swung the bike around, then headed back toward the main aisle, letting Cannon use up his last few shots. When he was sure Cannon couldn't fire again without reloading his gun, Jesse lined up Street Hawk with the main aisle and opened up the throttle. As he raced down the carpeted incline, filling the theatre with the roar of his engine, Jesse activated the vertical lift mechanism and catapulted into the air. There had been thousands of movies shown in that theatre over the past forty years, but never before had it been treated to the likes of Street Hawk's stunt leap, which carried Jesse all the way to the stage and brought him down amidst the carnage of shattered manikins and a few stray twenty-dollar bills.

'Thirty seconds, Jesse!' Norman beckoned.

Cannon had retreated to a corner of the backstage area, where he was fumbling with his gun, trying to feed a fresh round of ammunition into its cylinder. Jesse powered the bike forward and extended one leg out, kicking the gun from Cannon's hand and knocking the man down to the floor as he rode past. Cannon saw a length of pipe lying next to him, and he came up with it in his hand. As Jesse circled around to face him once more, Cannon let fly with the pipe, which narrowly missed catching both Jesse and the bike head-on.

'Jesse, get out of there! You're down to less than twenty seconds!'

'Not without him,' Jesse insisted.

'Eighteen seconds!' Norman yelped. 'Seventeen! Leave him be and go!'

Jesse inched his bike toward Cannon, who was verging on delirium as he crouched over the manikin with the money and tried to boost his take. 'You're finished,' Jesse told him. 'Give it up and get out.'

Cannon stared up wildly at Jesse, fearless and deranged. 'You don't get any of this! It's all mine!'

'Let him keep it, Jesse,' Norman hounded, 'Fourteen seconds, dammit!'

'This money is mine!' Cannon screamed, crumpling bills in his hands and rubbing them into his face. He was completely broken now, unhinged by the cumulative effect of the past few days and the intoxicating sight of the money.

'Forget it,' Jesse urged the man. 'This place is gonna blow. I can get you out. I want to see you on trial. . . .'

Cannon shook his head vigorously and staggered away from Jesse, still stuffing money into his coat. 'I can make it!' he wailed. 'I can make it!'

'Ten seconds!!' Norman screamed. 'Mach, move your butt!'

As Cannon leapt down from the stage and headed for one of the side-aisles, Jesse spun Street Hawk around so that he was facing the lobby.

'Seven . . . six.'

Jesse revved his engine and Street Hawk bolted down from the stage, landing harshly on the incline of the main aisle.

'Four . . . three . . . prepare for hyperthrust!!'

Jesse carefully continued up the aisle, lining up the front end of his bike so he could see the light pouring in through the lobby. There was nothing he could do about Cannon any more.

'Two . . . one . . . hyperthrust!'

As Jesse felt himself being dragged forward by the fierce propulsion of his bike, he could begin to hear the roar of explosive charges being detonated all around him. The sound grew to a loudness that surpassed that of any thunder he had ever heard. As he was speeding through the lobby, a shower of plaster rained down on him. Within seconds after he had cleared the theatre and reached the street, the Monarch Theatre began to crumble onto its foundation, like a castle made of cards that had just been hit by a sudden breeze. In quick succession, the adjacent buildings also rocked from the internal tumult of the detonations, and by the time Jesse had raced past the dumbfounded demolition crew and fled down the nearest alley, the entire block was in the process of flattening before the eyes of cheering onlookers and the lenses of the overhead cameras. From the perspective of the helicopters, Street Hawk had slipped clear of the destruction with the chilling grace of a bat out of hell. . . .

TWENTY

It was little over an hour after the block on Garland Boulevard had gone down in all its awe-inspiring glory. Jesse was seated at the same Venice café where he and Norman had eaten just prior to the whole chain of events that had begun with the arrival of the man pretending to be Detective Vincent Cannon. Although he sat calmly at his table, Jesse could feel a storm of emotion brewing beneath the drained numbness he'd experienced since escaping near-death at the Monarch Theatre. He absently ran his finger along the rim of his wine glass, trying to muster the thirst to have a drink and decide what he wanted to order. He didn't feel hungry, but he also knew he hadn't eaten all day and figured he should at least go through the motions while he worked his way through the troubling fog that seemed to enshroud him.

Norman had left the table more than five minutes before to use the washroom. Realizing how long he'd been away, Jesse finally looked over his shoulder to see if he could spot his missing friend. To his surprise, Jesse saw Norman standing at the bar, talking with the same blonde who had waited on them the last time they'd eaten here. Norman was smiling and talking with atypical animation, and the woman laughed lightly at whatever it was he had told her. She put a hand on Norman's forearm, then excused herself as the bartender summoned her over to pick up a round of drinks she had ordered. Taking a deep breath, Norman floated back to his seat, caught up in a cloud of his own.

'I don't believe you, Romeo,' Jesse told his friend. 'Was it just my imagination, or did you actually go through with it?'

Norman beamed with untold joy, then caught himself and tried to downplay his euphoria. It wasn't easy. 'Not only did I ask her out . . . she said "yes". And not only did she say "yes", but she also said she adores Stravinsky. *Adores*. Are you ready for that?'

'Are *you* ready, Norman?' Jesse said. '*That's* the question.'

'Absolutely. Imagine, a nice dinner before the show, orchestra seats for the performance . . . oh, I'm ready, all right.'

'Well, good for you, Norman.' Jesse raised his glass and proposed a toast. 'To Cupid and Eros, may they guide you well. . . .'

Norman blushed. 'Come on, Mach, it's only a date, for crying out loud! I mean, it's not like it's the first time for me.' They chinked glasses and slowly sipped their wine.

Jesse quickly lapsed back into his melancholy, and it didn't take Norman long to pick up on it. 'Still down on yourself, are you?'

Jesse sighed. 'Don't worry, I'll get over it.'

'Jess, you did all you could to save him.'

'I know. It's just that . . . something doesn't sit right with me about it all.'

'What do you mean?'

'It's hard to explain.' Jesse thought back over the confrontation in the theatre, then went on, 'You remember how he seemed to crack right at the end? Like he'd gone off the deep end . . .' Snapping his fingers, he added, 'Just like that. One second he was all there, concentrating on killing me . . . the next thing I know he's babbling like he's trying out for The Fool in some Shakespeare play.'

'It's been known to happen,' Norman said. 'Everybody

has their breaking point, they say. That was his.'

'Maybe so, but still . . .'

'It's done with, and that's what counts,' Norman insisted. 'Although, I would have liked to have known who he was. Not much chance of that, though. They'll be lucky if there's anything left of him in the rubble.'

'Norman, please . . .'

'Sorry.'

Jesse took another drink. On his empty stomach, the wine was taking quick effect, loosening him up slightly. 'We don't have to know *who* he was, I guess. We know *what* he was. That's enough.'

Norman nodded. 'More than enough.'

'So . . .' Jesse picked up his menu, changing the subject and trying to force a change in the mood. 'What are we eating today? I see there's a bargain-priced lunch Special with—'

'Nonsense, Jesse,' Norman interjected. 'Today it's top of the line. Best in the house, on me!'

Jesse blinked his eyes with wonder. 'Am I dreaming? Are you okay, Norman?'

'Perfectly.' With a happy grin, Norman turned and raised his hand to get the attention of the waitress, who had just finished taking an order at the nearest booth. 'Oh, Suzanne, love! We'd like to order now, *s'il vous plaît.*'

Jesse smirked as he rose from his seat. 'You're truly amazing, Norman, you ol' French dandy, you. Look, order me the shrimp cocktail and a bowl of soup. I have to call into the office. We're having a surprise birthday for Altobelli tomorrow and I'm in charge of the cake. . . .'

'How old is he?'

'Old enough not to let anyone know,' Jesse said as he turned to leave the table. He went inside the restaurant and used the phone in the men's room to put a call through to the station. When Rachel took his call, she delivered some news that had little to do with such trifles as a birthday cake. As he returned to his seat, Jesse had a strange look on his face.

'Norman . . . Cannon didn't die in the theatre. He managed to slip out the side entrance before the explosion. He's at the station now, under arrest. . . .'

TWENTY-ONE

'I still can't believe it!'

'Well, it's true, so you might as well get used to it,' Altobelli told Jesse, who'd just arrived at the station. They were in the commander's office, along with Rachel. Altobelli continued, 'Apparently Elkins had the money stashed somewhere in that theatre, and our man got his hands on some of it, then made a mad dash out the side door just as the place was blowing.'

'And he wasn't hurt?' Jesse asked, his mind reeling. He didn't see how it could have been possible.

Rachel explained, 'These demolition people have their act down, but good, Jesse. There were twenty-five buildings on that block, and every one of them fell straight down on itself with hardly any spillover. Cannon, or whatever his name turns out to be . . . he was in an alley no more than twenty feet wide, wedged between the theatre and a three-storey building. God knows how many tons of brick and steel collapsed on either side of him and he walked away with only a few bruises from a window frame that apparently bounded off the pavement and struck him as he was trying to make a run for it.'

Jesse shook his head. 'It's incredible.'

'You want to know something else that's incredible?' Altobelli said. 'The guy's got an accomplice, from the looks of things. You want to take a guess at who it is?'

'Who?'

'Street Hawk, that's who!' the commander snapped, bolting from his chair at the mere mention of his nemesis. 'According to witnesses, he zipped out of the theatre just before the explosion, too. Which means he had to be there with this Cannon impersonator. Which also means he's probably on the loose with a share of the money. Now, if I can only catch him, I'll finally have something better than speeding and obstructing justice to charge him with!'

'That reminds me, chief,' Rachel put in. 'I hate to say it, but the lobby's crawling with reporters. How do you think we should handle this?'

'Tell 'em "no comment"!' Altobelli snarled. 'Look, the guy isn't cooperating and we won't even know who the hell he is until we get a make on his prints!'

'Can I go ahead and at least say he's being held for arraignment in Elkins' death?' Rachel asked. 'That should be enough to get rid of most of them.'

'Yeah, do that.'

Rachel left the office, but Jesse stayed behind. He told Altobelli, 'I'd like to see him.'

'Yeah, I bet you would,' Altobelli said. 'But forget it. He's in solitary. We're hoping a little isolation might loosen his tongue.'

'Did he call a lawyer?'

'Maybe, maybe not.'

'Come again?'

Altobelli peeled an antacid tablet from its cellophane wrapper and slipped it into his mouth. 'He made a call, all right, but he didn't bother telling anybody who it was to. We assumed it was a lawyer, but we haven't heard from anyone. We're going to send him over to county this afternoon, let somebody else get headaches from him for a change.'

'How's he acting?' Jesse wanted to know.

'What do you mean?'

'Is he any different?'

Altobelli thought it over, then shook his head. 'No, not really. Well, maybe he's a little less cocky, being behind bars and all, but he's still not going to win any awards for charm, if that's what you're getting at. Why do you ask?'

'Just curious,' Jesse lied, backing up from the commander's desk. 'Well, I'm supposed to be off today. Now that this is all settled, is it all right if I leave?'

'Suit yourself,' Altobelli said.

As soon as Jesse left the squad room, he quickly detoured to the holding cells, convincing the officer on duty that he had Altobelli's clearance to see Cannon. Jesse found the would-be detective lying back on his cot in one of the smaller, isolated cells, staring at the ceiling. The crazed look that Jesse had seen on his face back at the Monarch was gone. If anything, Cannon appeared bored.

'So, "detective", we meet again,' Jesse called out through the bars.

Cannon craned his neck slightly to glance at Jesse, then he laid back, saying nothing.

'You played me for a chump, pal.'

'Who was playing?' Cannon sighed. 'You *are* a chump. I just took advantage of it.'

'How'd you get Elkins to talk before you killed him?'

'This isn't a courtroom, pal.'

'Aside from Elkins, you also killed the real Vincent Cannon. How many other murders do you have on your hands?'

Cannon sat up on his bunk and reached to his pocket for his cigarettes. 'I don't have to talk to you, Mach. Go take a powder.'

Jesse watched as the man lit his cigarette and laid back on the cot, blowing smoke rings as if he didn't have a care in the world. This hardly seemed to be the same man who, only a few hours before, had been smearing wads of money in his face and blathering like an idiot. As he left the holding cell area, Jesse's ears burned red with indignation. Cannon was right. He'd played Jesse for a chump, only Cannon didn't realize that the last time he'd done it had been in the Monarch Theatre.

TWENTY-TWO

The courtroom was only sparsely filled with onlookers when the impersonator of Vincent Cannon was brought in for his arraignment along with seven other offenders facing a variety of charges. Because no lawyer had turned up in response to Cannon's mysterious phone call, a legal counsel had been appointed for him, although he made no effort to cooperate in his own defence. In the hour and a half Cannon and his three-piece-suited advocate had been together, the only words the prisoner had bothered to utter were, 'I got nothing to say.' Accordingly, Cannon stood mute to the five charges pressed against him, the most serious being first-degree murder in the death of Mitch Elkins. The presiding judge ordered him to stand trial on all charges, then set Cannon's bail at four hundred and fifty thousand dollars and requested that he be incarcerated in the county jail pending a positive identification.

As the prisoner was being led from the defence desk to the side exit, a radiant, dark-haired woman stood up in the gallery and pointed a finger at Cannon. She was in her mid-thirties, dressed in the latest Paris fashions, and spoke with only the slightest South American accent as she accused, 'You killed the husband of my sister, you lowly dog. May the third sun of Charles strike you blind and—'

'Order!' the judge bellowed, banging his gavel. 'Order in the court!'

A security officer quickly moved down the aisle and grabbed the shrieking woman, who continued to stare at Cannon, wild-eyed. 'You're garbage! Rot in the smoke and tears of hell!'

'Get that woman out of here!' the judge demanded. 'And the same for the prisoner!'

Cannon watched as the woman was led away, then turned and allowed the bailiff to escort him out the side exit to where a police van was waiting to carry him and the other prisoners to the county jail. As he was ushered into the van and shackled to the riding bench, Cannon could no longer suppress a grin of admiration at the performance of the woman in the courtroom. Yes, she had been very convincing . . . and very eloquent, in her own way. As she had promised on the phone, she had succeeded in concocting a plan for his escape and relayed the news to him. What was it she had said? *May the third sun of Charles strike you blind*. At the intersection of Third and Charles Streets, he was to create a distraction for the driver of the police van. *You're garbage. Rot in the smoke and tears of hell.* That one was a little more difficult to decode, although he was fairly sure that smoke bombs and tear gas would be used as part of the escape plan. Perhaps the bombs would be set off in garbage cans near the intersection . . . he couldn't be sure. But then, that wasn't his concern. He just had to be ready when the time came.

It took another forty minutes for the rest of the prisoners to face up to their arraignments and to be returned to the van. Once everyone had been cuffed to the riding benches, the transport pulled away from the courthouse, with two guards riding in front and one officer remaining in back with the prisoners, armed with a nightstick and service revolver.

'Why all the glum faces, guys?' the officer taunted as he eyed his charges. 'It ain't like you're on your way to the gallows.'

'Hey,' one of the men snapped, 'you know what you can do with that nightstick?'

'Yeah,' the officer shot back. 'For starters, I can bust your kneecaps. Give me any more lip and I'll bust your chops, too!'

Leaning forward on the bench, Cannon was able to see a partial view of the street through an opening in the dividing wall between the front of the van and the back. They were heading down Charles Street and had just passed Second. It was time to act.

Joining in the argument, Cannon raised his voice and called the guard a few choice names to get his attention, then said, 'Yeah, you're a real big man, toting a gun and a club while you shoot your mouth off at guys with their hands tied behind their backs!'

'Shut up!' the officer warned him.

'And why don't you try to make me, pig-face!' Cannon struggled against his binds as he tried to get at the guard, who backed away and pulled his nightstick from its clip on his belt. The other prisoners picked up on Cannon's anger and added to the commotion with their own shouts and curses.

'What the hell's going on back there?' the driver said, glancing over his shoulder to see what was happening.

'Saunders, watch it!' the other officer in front shouted, drawing the driver's attention back to the road before them, where a garbage truck was backing out of an alley, blocking the street. Saunders had to slam on the brakes to avoid colliding with the larger vehicle.

'Moron!' Saunders yelled out his window as he pressed his palm against the horn. 'Why don't you watch where you're going!?'

The garbage truck backed the rest of the way out of the alley, then swung around so that it was facing the van. A large trash dumpster was poised on the front forks of the truck, and the moment the truck stopped, the dumpster lid swung open and two men dressed in commando fatigues popped up like lethal jack-in-a-boxes. Before Saunders and his partner could react, the commandos fired a pair of tear gas shells through the front windshield of the van. Instantaneously, an odious cloud of smoke bloomed inside the vehicle, seeping its way into the back area as well.

Holding his breath, Cannon smirked to himself. So far, so good. . . .

Eight miles away, Jesse was test-driving Street Hawk on an old stretch of gravel road running through the foothills of the San Gabriel Mountains. The area was relatively deserted, giving him plenty of room to try out a few manoeuvres and polish up on some of his off-road riding techniques. It was just the sort of break he needed after the Cannon-Elkins affair, and as he made a few vaulting jumps over dirt mounds and powered the bike up a perilously steep slope, Jesse felt his spirits had been adequately rejuvenated for the time being. He left the trails and rode onto a crest stretch of the mountain freeway, then started heading back into town.

Jesse hadn't travelled more than two miles when he spotted lights flashing in his rear-view mirror. The lights were soon accompanied by the howl of police sirens.

'Highway Patrol,' Jesse muttered to himself. 'Must be Holmes and Bellows. Why don't I make their day for them?'

'Why don't you not?' Norman's prating voice sounded inside of Jesse's helmet. 'Just ditch them and get back here.'

But Jesse kept down his speed, letting the patrol car gain ground on him. Once the gap between them had been closed to less than fifty yards, Jesse gently accelerated, signalling that the chase was on. When the police raised their speed to try to catch up, he opened up still more.

'Mach, this is not my idea of a good time.'

'Relax, Norman,' Jesse said as he leaned sharply to one side and took the corner in the road. 'I'm just having a little fun. I know these guys. They're lousy drivers. They'll never catch me.'

'I won't have you risking capture in the pursuit of kicks!' Norman retorted, 'Now, get your . . . wait a second! I'm getting an emergency assist call on police frequency, and it's not for you!'

'Better check it out,' Jesse said as he watched the digital readout on his speedometer climb to seventy-five miles an hour. The Highway Patrol was having a hard time keeping up with him on the winding turns of the freeway, but they weren't giving up the chase.

'Prison transport,' Norman reported to Jesse. 'Code Red. Say, wasn't that Cannon guy supposed to be arraigned and moved to county this afternoon?'

'Yes,' Jesse said. 'Get me the coordinates. I'm on my way.' Opening the throttle, Jesse gave Street Hawk a jolt of speed that quickly brought it over a hundred miles an hour, leaving the police cruiser far behind.

One by one, the prisoners stepped out of the fogged interior of the van, coughing and choking on the toxic cloud. The teary-eyed guard had his gun out and was barking commands to the men. 'Get out and form a tight circle to the right of the van! Anyone who gets any smart ideas is gonna regret it!'

Although the men had been disconnected from the van's benches, they still had their hands bound behind their backs. Cannon blinked the tears out of his eyes and remained inside the vehicle as long as he could, gesturing for others to leave ahead of him.

'What's your problem? You a glutton for punishment or something?' one of the men asked Cannon.

'Yeah, that's me,' Cannon coughed, stepping behind his fellow prisoner.

Meanwhile, Saunders and the other officer had drawn their guns and advanced on the stalled garbage truck. The driver had already fled, and after inspecting the cab, both men carefully climbed up onto the front bumper of the truck and grabbed hold of the lid to the dumpster. On a count of three, they raised the lid and pointed their guns inside.

'Freeze or you're dead!' Saunders shouted.

To the officer's amazement, however, he discovered that the dumpster was empty. The commandos were gone.

★

Inside a brown station wagon parked in an alley overlooking the intersection, two men watched the commotion taking place near the van. One of the men was dressed in combat fatigues similar to those of the missing commandos. The other man wore prison gear, and he also bore a chilling resemblance to the man who had been pretending to be Vincent Cannon. He had the same hulking build, the same drooping eyes, the same squat nose.

The man in the fatigues was behind the wheel, and from his perspective he had a clear view of the other commandos, who were hiding directly beneath the police van. Lifting a walkie-talkie to his lips, the driver waited until Saunders and his partner had climbed down from the garbage truck, then ordered, 'Smoke!'

Both men in the station wagon watched as one of the commandos pulled the pins on a pair of smoke bombs and tossed one out on either side of the van. The bombs exploded within seconds of one another, filling the air with a yellowish haze several times denser than that of the tear gas.

The driver turned to the man in the prison garb. 'Go!' When Cannon's lookalike hesitated, the driver shoved him slightly and whipped out a pistol. 'Move! Now!'

There was considerable confusion near the van as the twin clouds obscured things. The police officers quickly moved into position, forming a wide-gapped half-circle around the prisoners and threatening to shoot anyone who moved. Saunders issued an additional demand for the commandos to surrender themselves. Cannon realized that the police were too blinded by the smoke to effectively keep track of the situation, and the moment he climbed out of the van, he dropped to the ground and rolled under the vehicle, joining the two commandos. All three men traded quick nods of silent recognition as one of the commandos cut Cannon's binds from his wrists.

The smoke was beginning to dissipate, so Cannon quickly rolled out from under the van on the side away from the other prisoners. His lookalike was approaching through the haze, and they traded a brief glance before the other man moved off and circled around the back of the van to join the other prisoners. Cannon waited for the commandos to join him, then headed with them toward the alley where the station wagon was waiting.

Jesse arrived on the scene just as the prisoners were being led through the thinning smoke back into the van. He brought Street Hawk to a halt and waited for Norman to enhance the visibility range of his visor so that he could make out the prisoners.

'Looks like they have it under control,' Jesse reported. 'And there's Cannon just getting back in . . .'

'Jesse,' Norman interrupted. 'Look behind the van. Do you see—'

'Yes, I see them,' Jesse said, spotting Cannon and the commandos rushing toward the station wagon. With their backs turned to him, Jesse couldn't see who they were, but he quickly surmised, 'Must be some strays. I better show them the way back home.'

As the men piled into the station wagon, Cannon barked, 'Hit it before they wise up!'

The driver gunned the engine and took off down the alley, but one of the commandos quickly realized that they hadn't made a clean getaway. Staring out the back of the vehicle, he reported, 'Biker on our rear flank.'

Jesse emerged through the dying smoke like an apparition, bearing down quickly on the getaway car. Cannon couldn't believe that his arch-foe could have shown up yet another time to give him grief.

'Take him out!' he told the commandos angrily. 'I want him dead!'

The commandos clearly were under Cannon's control now that he was free, and the man who had spotted Jesse swiftly grabbed a pair of phosphorus grenades, keeping one and handing the other to his partner. They both rolled down their windows and flung the grenades back in the direction of Street Hawk. Instead of smoke, these explosives gave off a blazing, widespread curtain of flame that effectively blocked the entire alley. Jesse had to apply the air foils to bring Street Hawk to a stop less than a few feet from the searing flames.

'What are you waiting for?' Norman asked Jesse.

'Norman, can't you see? That's a damn wall of fire! You trying to get me killed?'

'Street Hawk can withstand temperatures of up to two thousand degrees,' Norman reminded Jesse.

'Great. What about me?'

'Your suit's fireproof. Now, go!'

Jesse took a deep breath. 'What ever happened to your sense of caution about your bike, Norman?'

'Go!'

Jesse opened the throttle and stood Street Hawk up on its rear wheel as he sped through the flaming obstacle, emerging just in time to see the brown station wagon cut sharply to the right at the end of the alley. Jesse sped even faster, trying to catch up, and only well-honed reflexes prevented him from slamming into the side of a delivery truck that suddenly moved out into the alley from a side drive. With a quick activation of the vertical lift mechanism, Jesse was able to hurdle the truck and skid to a stop at the end of the alley. However, he soon realized that the alley gave way to a busy street, and in the dense flow of traffic, there was no trace of the station wagon.

'Oh, that's just great,' Jesse muttered. He gave himself a quick onceover to make sure he wasn't on fire, then sighed and waited for a break in traffic so he could leave the alley behind. His bolstered spirits were already beginning to sag.

TWENTY-THREE

The sectioned billboard posted on the outside wall of the warehouse serving as Street Hawk's operational headquarters parted in the middle as Jesse pulled into the back alley, and by way of another jolt of the bike's vertical lift, he was able to neatly fly up through the opening and roll down the jettison chute into the holding area. Norman bounded out of his chair in front of the command module and strode excitedly over to where Jesse was removing his helmet.

'What a run!' he gasped. 'Mach, that was fantastic! Absolutely top-drawer!'

Norman's ebullience was in sharp contrast to Jesse's low spirits. As he climbed off the bike and tried to stretch some of the stiffness out of his arms and legs, Jesse deadpanned, 'Norman, the station wagon got away, in case you've forgotten.'

'True,' Norman conceded, 'but you passed the heat resiliency test with flying colours. Admit it, you didn't feel a thing when you were going through those flames, did you?'

Jesse handed his helmet to Norman and trudged his way to the exercise room, where he began climbing out of his form-fitting racing suit. 'Tuttle, I know we're a team, but sometimes I wonder if we're playing the same game.'

'Sure we are. We're just playing with my ball.' Norman grinned with satisfaction. 'And my rules.'

'Yeah, right.' Jesse stepped into the shower and shouted over the gush of hot water, 'You know, I'm beginning to think I shouldn't have pushed you into dating, Norman. You get your girl to agree to go out with you to some highbrow concert and all of a sudden you go around with a swelled head, looking like the cat who just polished off the canary.'

'What can I say?' Norman gloated happily as he began his routine post-ride inspection of Street Hawk, humming a passage from his favourite Stravinsky composition.

Jesse remained in the shower until the water began to change temperature. The massage setting on the shower head had done wonders for soothing the muscular aches Jesse was feeling from the past few days of riding. As he stepped out of the stall and towelled off, Jesse inspected the prosthesis that now constituted his right knee. He was amazed at how well the part was holding up and enabling him to partake in all the things, particularly riding, that had been denied him following the accident in the desert several months ago that had left him lame in that one leg. Having to play ball by Norman's eccentric rules seemed like a small price to pay for the new lease on life the prosthesis had given him.

By the time Jesse had changed and come out of the exercise room, Norman's cheerful disposition had changed dramatically. He was no longer humming Stravinsky, much less even grinning. A scowl was pressed across his face as he tinkered with the front end of the bike.

'Seeya around, Norman. I think I'm going to head home and—'

'Don't leave just yet, Mach,' Norman said. 'Get over here. I want you to see this.'

'See what?'

When Jesse had joined his associate, Norman pointed at the bike and said, with a layer of irritation in his voice, 'Look at that, would you?'

Jesse looked and shrugged his shoulders. 'You shined it up real nice, as usual, Norman. Thanks. I appreciate it.'

'I'm talking about the wheel!' If Norman's right hand had been a gun, the finger he was pointing would be firing rounds into the bike's front tyre. 'Look at the wheel, Mach!'

Jesse eyed Norman warily, then leaned over and squeezed the tyre. 'Feels like thirty pounds of pressure to me. What seems to be the problem here?'

'Not *seems*,' Norman said. '*Is*. Here *is* the problem, right on the Magnum spoke.'

'Oh.' Jesse leaned his head close to the wheel and squinted. 'What am I looking for, Norman? Or am I supposed to take three guesses?'

'Don't you see it?'

'What?'

'The crack, Mach. The crack!'

Jesse ran his finger over the area in question, then stared hard at it again. 'Sorry, Norman, but I don't see it.'

'Of course you don't!' Norman exclaimed with annoyance. 'It's not visible to the naked eye.'

'Not visible to the—'

'The calibrator picked it up as I was checking out the front end. You probably did it when you made that reckless jump over the delivery truck in that alley.'

'Reckless?' Jesse questioned, taking a step back from the bike. 'Wait just a minute here, Norman. You were beaming from ear to ear when I came back. You said I was fantastic, that I—'

'I said the run was fantastic,' Norman corrected.

'Oh, I get it. The run was fantastic, but I, who made the run, wasn't so hot. . . .'

'Please, please try to understand,' Norman pleaded with what little patience he could muster. 'Street Hawk is a very delicate machine. You're going to have to learn how to handle vertical lift more carefully. You're not on the motor-cross circuit any more. You can't beat this machine . . . you have to caress it.'

Jesse rolled his eyes. 'What are we talking about here? A motorcycle or a dancing partner?'

'In some ways, you have to handle one like the other,' Norman insisted. 'I mean, you wouldn't drop your date on the floor when you dip her, would you?'

'Dip? I don't dip when I dance, Norman.' Jesse put on his coat and started for the door. 'And let me give you some advice. I doubt that your blonde friend from the restaurant dips when she dances, either. . . .'

'I'm taking her to a concert, not a dance!' Norman said. 'Where are you going?'

'There's a ballgame and a good late show on the tube,' Jesse said. 'I'm going to buy a sub sandwich, a bag of chips, and a six-pack of beer and plant myself in front of the television until all they're showing is test patterns, *that's* where I'm going. . . .!'

TWENTY-FOUR

The late show Jesse stayed up to watch starred George Hamilton as Evil Knievel, one of Jesse's childhood heroes and rôle models during his early years on the motorcross circuit. Having already seen the movie four times, he knew how godawful it was, but there were some good bike stunts that he would never get tired of watching. It was after one when he turned in for the night, falling into a deep slumber brought on by a combination of physical exhaustion and the lulling effects of six beers. He had a series of strange dreams, most of them featuring the Monarch Theatre, dismembered manikins, and the leering presence of the mysterious killer who had impersonated Vincent Cannon. And yet, oddly enough, when the alarm went off at seven o'clock, Jesse awoke thinking about the chocolate cake he had forgotten to get for Commander Altobelli's birthday. Fortunately, there was a bakery on the way to work with a reputation for cakes and Jesse was able to pick up a three-layer special and a fresh croissant for breakfast and still manage to show up at work a couple minutes early.

Bernie Goldberg, the lab technician, rubbed his hands together with expectation when he saw Jesse bring the cake in.

'Oh, that's going to be perfect! Just leave it in the lab so I can put the final touches on it!'

'What final touches?' Jesse asked, finishing his croissant.

Bernie arched his eyebrows deviously and reached into the pockets of his lab jacket, coming up with eight rolls of antacid tablets. 'I'm going to spell out "HAPPY BIRTHDAY" with these. After his press conference, the chief's gonna need 'em.'

'Is that where he is now?'

Bernie nodded as he led Jesse down the hall and opened the door to his lab so the cake could be brought inside.

'We're going to present him with the cake during lunch-break, so try to hang around the office for a change, okay?'

'I'll try,' Jesse said. 'But no promises.'

'You know, I can't figure it out, Mach. I never saw a PR man spend as much time out of the office as you do. When are we going to see some results? Hells bells, ever since Street Hawk showed up, the Department's been coming up with black eyes right and left.'

'Hey, I'm not a street cop these days, Bernie. There's not much I can do about Street Hawk.' It was all Jesse could do to keep a straight face. 'I'm going to check in on the chief.'

Altobelli was bracing up under his usual grilling in the press room, standing behind the podium as if it were a magical barrier that could keep not only reporters, but also their questions from getting to him. Things didn't work that way, however, and he was forced to fend off the media's assault with his usual rejoinder.

'No comment.'

'Come on, Commander,' a reporter in the front row complained. 'Give us a break here, okay? Street Hawk bailed out the police half a dozen times this past week, and now you're trying to trump up some half-baked charge against him. I mean, is the police force really *that* jealous of this guy that they'd stoop to get him out of the way?'

'No comment.' Altobelli glanced over at Rachel out of the corner of his eye. She was standing behind him and off to one side, carrying the latest news packets to be handed out following the press conference. There was nothing she felt she could say, so she returned a slight shrug of her shoulders.

Another of the reporters raised his hand and called out, 'You claim that Street Hawk was a possible accessory to the guy who was pretending to be a detective, and yet the only real connection you've made between them is that they were both at the Monarch Theatre just before it blew up. Isn't it likely that Street Hawk was there to apprehend the guy instead of help him?'

'We intend to ask him that once he's in custody,' Altobelli said.

Jesse wove his way through the reporters and joined Rachel near the podium. 'Bernie's got the cake,' he whispered in her ear above the drone of questions coming from the media mob. 'How're things here?'

'See for yourself,' Rachel told him, taking a step away from the Commander so she and Jesse could speak more freely. 'All the press wants to talk about is Street Hawk, and Altobelli's about to blow his cool.'

One of the local stations' most prominent anchorwomen was on hand for a rare assignment. She raised her distinctive voice to make sure she was heard above the din. 'Commander Altobelli, I think the basic issue here is that Street Hawk's embarrassing your entire department and you're trying to malign him to save face.'

'I really don't care what you think,' Altobelli shot back. 'Look, can we discuss something besides Street Hawk?'

Jesse shook his head and whispered to Rachel, 'Poor guy. What a way to have to start out a birthday.'

Ignoring Altobelli's plea, another reporter shouted, 'Do you have any definite plans for catching Street Hawk? We understand his bike is fast beyond belief and that it easily outran a Highway Patrol vehicle giving chase only yesterday afternoon.'

'This is the Police Department, not the Highway Patrol,' the Commander reminded the reporter. 'As for the first part of your question, which is going to be the last one I address regarding Street Hawk . . . at the moment, there are discussions going on between myself, the mayor's office, and several other law enforcement agencies. Including the

Highway Patrol, if you must know. Our consensus is that it's only a matter of time before we have this two-wheeled scourge off the streets and behind bars.'

The anchorwoman, playing to her cameraman, wise-cracked, 'Commander, isn't that the same thing the Sheriff of Nottingham said about Robin Hood?'

There was an outburst of chuckles and chortles amidst the press corps, and Altobelli turned away from them, glaring at Rachel and Jesse. 'I don't need this aggravation. Why do I keep putting myself through it?'

Rachel smiled bleakly and suggested, 'It's all in the line of duty, chief.'

Jesse seconded the assessment, adding, 'You do it because you're your own man and you don't want anybody else speaking for you on behalf of the Department.'

'Yeah,' Altobelli agreed half-heartedly. 'This is what I get for being so damn high and mighty, I guess.'

When the Commander turned back to face the press, a reporter asked him, 'Is there any more information you can give us concerning the attack on that prison transport van this morning?'

Behind the chief, Rachel muttered, 'Finally. Something Street Hawk wasn't in on.'

Jesse kept silent, smiling slightly to himself.

'I don't have a full report,' Altobelli told the media, 'but from the information that has come in so far, the attack was apparently made by terrorists of what looked to be South American nationality. It's sheer speculation at this time, but we're acting on the premise that they were hoping to free some of the prisoners, perhaps to recruit for their own organization.'

'And did any of the prisoners escape?'

'No,' Altobelli insisted. 'All the prisoners have been accounted for. The terrorists were apparently scared off before they could carry out what they had started. . . .'

Jesse's jaw dropped slightly at Altobelli's statement. Something wasn't right.

Altobelli quickly wrapped up the press conference and excused himself. As Rachel went to the front doorway and passed out press releases to the departing reporters, Jesse took off after the Commander, catching up to him in the squad room.

'Excuse me, Commander. About the press conference . . .'

Altobelli wandered into his office and headed for the water cooler. 'I know, I blew it,' he said sourly as he plopped a seltzer tablet into a cup of water and watched it begin to dissolve. 'This whole Street Hawk thing is beginning to get to me. We have to turn it around, Mach.'

'Yes, sir, but I was wondering—'

'Take the offensive,' Altobelli interrupted, brainstorming aloud. 'Maybe offer a reward.'

'Sir, I don't think a reward is such a good idea.'

Altobelli took a sip from his cup. 'You're right. Too close to Robin Hood.' The Commander went over to his desk and slumped down in his chair. 'Look, Mach, you and Rachel get to work on it. Come up with something we can use. Psychological profile . . . anything. I want to know what makes that guy tick!'

'I'll see what I can do, chief.' Jesse waited a moment for Altobelli to finish his drink, then said, 'About that transport hit this morning . . .'

'What about it, Mach?'

'You told the press no one escaped.'

Altobelli nodded and picked up a file from his desk. 'Here, it's all in the report. A big mess, but no one was hurt and no one got away.'

'Do you think the report might be in error?'

'How do you mean?'

'I don't know,' Jesse mused. 'Maybe somebody escaped and they're trying to keep a lid on it.'

'They?' Altobelli drawled sarcastically. 'I got news for you, Mach. *They* are *us*, and if anybody escaped, *we'd* be out there looking for him. Why the doubts?'

'Just the cop in me, I guess,' Jesse shrugged. 'From what I've heard, it seemed like a well-executed assault. It doesn't make sense that they had everything set up and then just disappeared instead of following through. It seems like at least somebody must have gotten away.'

Altobelli leaned back in his chair and eyed Jesse. 'This another one of your psychic hunches, Mach? Is that it, huh?'

'Yeah, maybe something like that.'

'Well, if it'll make you feel any better, why don't you look into it? And while you're at it, why don't you put some of your voodoo to work in getting a bead on Street Hawk?'

Jesse laughed lightly. 'I'll see what I can do.'

Before Jesse could leave, Officer Farnsworth rapped his knuckles on the doorframe and stepped in, carrying a manila envelope, which he handed to Altobelli. 'We finally got a make on the guy who killed Cannon and Elkins. You're gonna be surprised. Turns out *his* name is Cannon, too, if you can believe that.'

Farnsworth left the office as Jesse circled around the desk so he could look over Altobelli's shoulder at the identification documents.

'Well, I'll be . . .' Altobelli mused. 'Name's Jake Cannon. No relation to the guy he killed though . . . a professional mercenary, eh? Stints in Chile, Argentina, Bolivia, San Leandro . . . guy got around.'

Jesse quickly put two and two together. 'Chief, didn't that report on the transport hit say the terrorists were South American?'

'Yeah, as a matter of fact, it did. Hmm, you think it was an attempt to spring Cannon?'

'I'd bet on it,' Jesse said, thinking back to the incident at Third and Charles. He could have sworn that he had seen Cannon being led back into the van, but then who was the prisoner that got away? It didn't make sense.

Altobelli skimmed through more of the information and pointed his finger at a section of the printout. 'Aha! And here's where he links up with Elkins. When he was doing mercenary work in San Leandro, he was bankrolled by Big Stan Girard.'

'The same Girard who runs the cocaine racket here?' Jesse speculated.

'The same. San Leandro probably has its share of coca plants, making it worth Girard's while to get involved in their politics. He probably used Cannon down there and liked the results, then brought him up to go after Elkins.' Altobelli smiled for the first time all day. 'Well, now, it looks like we've got our hands on somebody even higher up than Elkins. If we can get Cannon to talk, who knows, we might be able to not only wrap up the stink with Dale and Cummings, but also get some goods on Girard.'

'Yeah, that'd be great, chief,' Jesse concurred. He was still plagued by doubts regarding the current status of Cannon, and he wanted to look into the matter as soon as possible.

There was a sudden commotion out in the squad room, and when Altobelli and Jesse looked to see what was happening, the first thing they noticed was the birthday cake Rachel was carrying into the office. Behind her was half the department, all joining in on a horrendous rendition of 'Happy Birthday'.

'Hey, what d'ya know,' Altobelli said, grinning at the cake. 'You turkeys remembered . . . oh, and what's this? Oh, now that's a real laugh, gang.' He peeled one of the antacid tablets out of the cake's frosting and popped it in his mouth, accompanied by a bevy of cheers from his underlings.

'Speech! Speech!' Bernie called out.

As Altobelli stood up and cleared his throat, trying to think up an appropriate anecdote, Jesse worked his way to the back of the crowd and then slipped out of the squad room. In all the excitement, he didn't figure he'd be missed, and there were certain pressing matters that he wanted to tend to, the most important of which was a trip to the county jail.

TWENTY-FIVE

Jesse put a quick call through to Norman before leaving the station, informing his associate about the identity of Jake Cannon and asking Norman to see if he could find out any further information on the mercenary. While Jesse was at the county jail, Norman went to work with his computers, tapping various intelligence sources to come up with a portfolio on Cannon that surpassed the thumbnail background sketches that had ended up in Commander Altobelli's hands. Norman was compiling the data into one comprehensive program when Jesse showed up, looking fit to be tied.

'Hey, I didn't figure to see you for at least another hour, Mach.'

'Yeah, well my visit at the jail was a short one,' Jesse said, pounding his fist against the wall with frustration.

'What's the matter?' Norman asked. 'What happened?'

Jesse came over to the command module. 'If you can believe this,' he said, his voice thick with cynicism, 'there was a flash fire in the prison kitchen just before I got there. They pulled one body out of the rubble, and it was burned beyond recognition, but according to the warden, it was—'

'—Cannon?' Norman guessed. 'I don't buy it.'

'Neither did I,' Jesse said. 'I asked to see the body, but it had already been picked up by the coroner. The warden insists they pulled prints off the corpse and made a positive ID of Cannon.'

'Going on the premise that the real Cannon got away,' Norman surmised, 'that's an awfully convenient string of coincidences putting him out of the picture.'

'Isn't it, though. I tried to suggest that maybe somebody had tampered with the fingerprints, but the warden blew a gasket and had me thrown out.'

'Probably just a matter of ego for him. I doubt that he was directly involved in a cover-up.' Norman turned to his computers. 'Girard no doubt has his own network of heavies inside the prison. When Cannon's stand-in was admitted, he was as good as dead.'

'Yeah, that's the way I see it, too.' Jesse looked at the monitor screens. 'What did you come up with on your end? Any good clues on where the real Cannon might have escaped to?'

'I think so.' Norman punched up the file on Cannon, referring to it as he spoke. 'Mostly I came up with the same stuff you got at the station. Soldier of fortune, specializing in South American politics. Heaviest involvement in San Leandro. Girard put him there, but it looks like Cannon set up a pretty strong allegiance with the Preveras while he was working for them.'

'Political Science isn't my strong suit, Norman,' Jesse confessed. 'Fill me in.'

Norman flashed a map of South America up on one of the monitor screens. 'That's San Leandro up in the corner of Bolivia, right near Brazil's hill farms. It's a small country. Dabbles with coffee exports for show, but their real claim to fame is cocaine production. Their hills are crawling with it, and the hills are government owned. At the time Cannon was down there, a couple years back, the Preveras were in power. Edmond and Simone. They pressed the lower classes into forced labour camps up in the hills, helping line their coffers by cultivating the coca plants. Cannon came into the picture when the peasants started revolting. He headed up a counter-revolutionary militia and was doing a good job until he was lured away from the capital to flush out some commandos in the hills. Turns out it was a false alarm, and while Cannon was away, revolutionaries stormed the capital and took over. Edmond and his entire staff were killed, but Simone managed to get out, along with a few loyal supporters. Word is she's hiding out here in the States, trying to put together the means of going back down and reclaiming control of the government.'

'Which means she was probably behind Cannon's escape,' Jesse said. 'We have to find her.'

'I tried,' Norman confessed.'The State Department, the Pentagon, Immigration, CIA, Interpol. Nobody has a current address on her.'

'What about DMV?'

'The Department of Motor Vehicles?' Norman said. 'You can't be serious!'

'Try it, Norman.'

Norman sighed and attacked the computer keyboard once again, querying the DMV for any information on vehicles owned by one Simone Prevera. The computers hummed for several seconds, then the monitor lit up like a Vegas slot machine touting a jackpot.

SIMONE PREVERA
Vehicle Registration number 109635F
Vehicle Registration number 109673E
Vehicle Registration number 112634J
Vehicle Registration number 113743Q
Vehicle Registration number 121234H
Vehicle Registration number 109674Q
Expiration Date 7 June 1986
Current address 40 Shore Cove Drive
Malibu, CA

'Amazing,' Norman exclaimed.

'It's an old police trick,' Jesse told Norman on his way to the door. 'Everybody owns a car.'

'Or, in her case, six. . . .'

TWENTY-SIX

Simone Prevera's Malibu residence was highlighted by a lavish Mediterranean-style villa built on a bluff overlooking the Pacific. Tall palms swayed in the ocean breeze all around the walled-in property, and the landscaped grounds were alive with a blaze of colour from bougainvillea, azalea, birds-of-paradise, and other blooming plants. Jesse took this all in as he slowly drove up the winding asphalt driveway. In addition to the armed guard who had let him past the wrought-iron gates when he had flashed his police credentials, Jesse also spotted one other security officer roaming the grounds. He suspected there were probably other gunmen he couldn't see. All in all, it looked as if Simone Prevera was living out her exile in a state of secure luxury.

Next to the villa was an elongated garage filled with the cars that had tipped off Jesse to Simone's address in the first place. She had quite a collection. A Cadillac, two Mercedes, a BMW, a Rolls Royce, and a Corvette Stingray—each vehicle freshly waxed and gleaming in its parking space. Jesse made a mental note that he would have to wash his Mustang soon, then pulled to a stop in front of the villa.

The guard at the gate had apparently relayed news of Jesse's arrival, because just as Jesse was getting out of his car, Simone Prevera stepped out of the front door and headed down the steps to greet him. She was the same woman who had confronted Jake Cannon in the courtroom the day before, advising him of the nature of his pending escape attempt. Instead of her Paris ensemble, however, she was dressed down in a flower-print silk kimono that clung enticingly to her voluptuous figure.

'Officer Mach, is it?' she inquired graciously, holding out her hand.

'That's correct, ma'am.' Jesse shook her hand and showed his credentials. 'I was wondering if I could just have a minute of your time.'

'But of course.' Simone smiled, fluttering her long dark eyelashes. 'I always have time for a man of the law . . . especially when that man has charm and the looks of a matinée idol. Please, come inside. Let me fix you something to drink.'

'No, thanks.' Up on the roof of the villa, Jesse glimpsed still another armed man pacing along a catwalk connecting the main building with servants' quarters. 'I just wanted to ask you a few questions about a man called Jake Cannon. I believe he was in your employ during you and your husband's reign in San Leandro. . . .'

'That's correct,' Simone replied calmly, 'although I don't know that there is much I can tell you. I have not seen him since the coup, and that was more than two years ago. If I never see him again, I will be glad.'

Jesse noted the look of anger that had crept into Simone's features. 'I'm surprised,' he told her. 'I was under the impression he was a friend.'

'Was,' Simone said. 'But no longer. In the end, he betrayed us. I hold him responsible for my husband's death.'

'How would you feel if I told you Jake Cannon was dead?'

Simone's eyes were still clouded with rage, but Jesse's news seemed to placate her somewhat. Her anger passed, giving way to the same cordial ease that had marked her demeanour when Jesse had first seen her.

'If Jake Cannon is dead, that is a good thing,' she said. 'You will forgive my lack of grief, but I will not shed tears for the man who sought my ruin. I may be many things, Officer Mach, but I am not a sentimental fool.'

'I'm sure you're right, Ms Prevera. Now, if you will excuse me. . . .'

'Simone,' the woman insisted. 'You must call me Simone, and there is no need for you to leave so soon. I will be having lunch soon. You must join me.'

'Thanks, but I can't,' Jesse apologized. 'I have other matters to tend to. I appreciate your time, and I'm sorry to have bothered you.'

'It was no bother at all, believe me,' Simone said with a coquettish flair in her voice. 'Officer Mach, do you dance?'

Jesse stopped next to his Mustang and looked back at the woman. 'A little, but not much,' he told her. 'I've had some knee problems of late.'

'What a shame,' Simone sniffed, letting her gaze roam up and down Jesse. 'You have a perfect body for the tango. . . .'

Jesse blushed and quickly slipped inside his Mustang. Simone remained in front of the villa, watching him pull away, a flirtatious smile still sliced across her olive-skinned face. Once the car was out of sight, however, she stopped smiling and returned inside the house, making her way past an ornately-decorated living room and den to a bedroom, where a stocky, elderly man was giving a massage to Jake Cannon. Simone waved the older man away, then poured a light layer of oil onto her fingers before moving in to continue Cannon's massage.

'Oh, that feels great. Just like old times,' Cannon moaned contentedly.

When Cannon tried to reach for Simone's leg, she swatted his hand away. 'There'll be plenty of time for that later. Right now we have things to do. The police have begun to sniff, so we must move quickly. . . .'

TWENTY-SEVEN

They drove to Long Beach in the Rolls Royce. Simone was at the wheel, eyes hidden behind a pair of dark-lensed designer sunglasses. Cannon sat across from her, one arm hanging out of the window as he stared idly at the traffic they kept passing as they made their way down the Golden State Freeway. Salsa music blared over the expensive sound system, and Cannon drummed his fingers on the roof of the Rolls to the beat.

'What a great day to be out of the slammer!' he said. 'I tell ya, Simone, you need to get yourself a limo and a decent chauffeur. Just think, we could be riding in the back seat right now, sipping Dom Perignon and catching up on some old times, if you know what I mean. . . .'

When Cannon's left hand wandered over the stick shift and headed for Simone's lap, she smiled, but at the same time swatted it away, telling him, 'I do my own driving because it puts me in control. I lost my country by letting too many other people make decisions on my behalf.'

'You aren't talking about me, I trust.'

'No, Jake,' she said, still smiling. 'You were the one man I could trust . . . even more than my own husband. That's one of the reasons I went to so much trouble to see that you were released from prison.'

Cannon lowered the volume on the radio. 'And another reason has something to do with this boat you're taking me to see, right?'

Simone nodded. 'Yes, it is the key to the new revolution.'

'Want to be more specific?'

'We'll be there soon enough.'

Simone veered off onto the Harbour Freeway, which would take them to San Pedro and then Long Beach. Cannon lit up a cigarette, then reached inside his coat pocket for a silver drinking flask. He unscrewed the cap and helped himself to a long, warm swallow of Scotch, then smacked his lips with satisfaction.

'You heard from Mr Girard lately, Simone?' he asked.

'No, I haven't,' she replied bitterly. 'He is a chauvinist pig! He dealt only with my husband. You know that. He had eyes for me, but only seeking pleasure. When I came to him after the overthrow, looking for his support, he said that he would help only if he could choose a man to run the country . . . and if I would be his mistress. I spat in his face and that was the end of that. Why do you ask? Do you still feel a loyalty to him?'

'Hardly,' Cannon said. 'After what happened to Elkins and all that money, it's just as well that Mr Girard believes I died in that prison fire.'

'There's a chance that he might try to intervene once I've regained the throne in San Leandro,' Simone speculated.

'If we can do without him, I'll just take him out if he gets in the way,' Cannon promised.

'I was hoping you would say that, Jake.' Simone drove over the Vincent Thomas Bridge, which spanned the Los Angeles Main Channel and brought them to the periphery of the Long Beach Navy Yard. Rather than pass through the tollgate to get closer to the harbour, Simone turned the Rolls down a side street and parked alongside the curb at a spot where they had a view of the west basin of the shipyard. Getting out of the car, Simone took a pair of binoculars out of their carrying case and looked through them momentarily before handing them to Cannon. 'It's the last ship on the right.'

Cannon adjusted the sights on the binoculars as he gazed down at the shipyard. 'Number four fifty-three? The troop carrier?'

'Yes, that's the one,' Simone confirmed. 'It's carrying twenty million dollars-worth of San Leandran currency, still negotiable in the States.'

Cannon let out a low whistle as he lowered the binoculars. 'That's a lot of bread, Simone. How'd you pull that off?'

'The ship was on loan to us from the American government,' Simone explained. 'When I began to suspect an overthrow in my country, I secretly withdrew much of the money from our treasury and transferred it to the ship, knowing that it would be seized by your Navy in the event of a revolution and brought back here safely. I never could have smuggled that much money out of the country any other way.'

'How come nobody ever found it?'

Simone grinned. 'As I told the police officer earlier, I am not a fool. I had the currency placed between the inner and outer hulls, then had the aft voids welded shut in a way that wouldn't draw suspicion.'

'Smart lady,' Cannon admitted. 'So you've got yourself a king-sized floating safe.'

When Cannon took out his cigarettes, Simone gestured for one of them. Blowing smoke, she said, 'My only problem is that I don't have access to the ship now. I need to get the money out. Can you help me, Jake?'

Cannon looked back at the shipyard, letting twin trails of smoke spill from his nostrils. When he turned back to Simone, he was ready to negotiate. 'Of course I could . . . if it was worth my while.'

'You would be paid handsomely,' Simone assured him. 'With that much money, I could finance an effective revolution and put myself back in power. This time, I would not have my husband to work around. I would be Queen, and I would make the right decisions to see that there would be no insurgency.'

'And you would be in need of a King, perhaps?' Cannon suggested. 'Or at least a Prime Minister?'

'I will run the country alone,' Simone insisted. 'But you could have your pick of any position under me.'

Cannon leered suggestively at Simone. 'Any position?'

Simone laughed. 'You have an impure mind, Jake.'

'It's all your fault, Simone. You lead me astray.'

Simone fielded Cannon's hungry gaze, then told him, 'Let us tend to business before we turn our minds to pleasure, Jake. There is much to be done, and we don't have much time to do it. You see, the Navy has ordered our ship to be used for target practice, because it is so obsolete. We have only twenty-four hours to get to the money. . . .'

TWENTY-EIGHT

'Well, well, if it isn't the reincarnation of Harry Houdini himself,' Rachel drawled as she ran into Jesse in the hallway of the police station. 'Where'd you disappear to this time? Or is that none of my business, even if I'm technically supposed to be your immediate superior?'

'Sorry, Rachel,' Jesse apologized. 'But, uh, the chief wanted me to look into some background material that might give us some leads on Street Hawk. He said it's supposed to be top priority, so I—'

'Never mind,' Rachel said, walking away from Jesse. 'I don't want to hear it.'

'Rachel, I . . .' Jesse saw her disappear inside her office and slam the door shut behind her. He deliberated about trying to smooth things over with her, but decided there wasn't much he could say that would change things. He knew that the only way he'd ever end up on a good standing with Rachel would be to abandon his Street Hawk duties and concentrate fully on public relations work, which wasn't an idea that appealed to him. Instead, he proceeded to the squad room and made his way through the maze of desks to Altobelli's office, where he found the Commander sitting behind his desk, eating what was left of his birthday cake.

'This is killing me, but what a way to go,' Altobelli said between bites. 'I'm glad you dropped in, Mach. We have to talk about something.'

'Well, that makes it unanimous, chief,' Jesse replied, 'because I was wondering if you could lend me a little bit of clout in trying to get some info on the guy who was burned to death over at the jail this morning. You've heard about it, I assume. . . .'

'Oh, I've heard about it, all right,' Altobelli said. 'I was in the middle of my birthday celebration when I got a call from Warden Cameron. He was close to foaming at the mouth over certain accusations you were making.'

'Well, sir, it's just that I find it hard to believe Cannon could have ended up killed in such a fluke accident, especially when—'

'Look, Mach, I know I told you to look into this thing with Cannon, but now, fluke or not, he's dead and so is the whole issue concerning him. We're just going to have to nab somebody else to get the information we're looking for, that's all.'

'But, chief, I'm telling you, I don't think the guy that died was really Cannon. Now, if I could just have a look at the body—'

'Forget it!' Altobelli shovelled the last piece of cake into his mouth and washed it down with a sip of seltzer water. 'Let me paint you a picture. Warden Cameron and I are not what you would call bosom buddies. What's worse, he and a lot of his friends have ways of making my life miserable if they think I'm trying to do the same to them, which is the idea they got when you went over there stirring things up this morning. So as far as I'm concerned, and as far as *you* are concerned, Mach, Cannon died in that fire and that's that. I want you to drop it, period. Forget I ever mentioned looking into it. You have some nervous energy to work off, spend it on trying to help us get our hands on Street Hawk. Is that clear?'

Jesse wanted to protest, but he thought better of it.

'Yes, sir,' he replied with a sigh, turning to leave the office.

'And, Mach,' Altobelli added. 'In case you get any ideas . . . I had Cannon's body red-tagged. If you go near it, I'll find out, and I won't be happy.'

'Yes, sir.'

'Now get back to work.'

'Yes, sir.' Jesse started out the door, then paused long enough to glance back and say, 'Oh, and Happy Birthday, sir.'

'Thanks, Mach. You want to give me a present, do what I say and keep your nose clean.'

Jesse nodded, but he only managed to keep his nose clean for the few minutes it took him to reach the downstairs laboratory, where he found Bernie Goldberg looking over a cement cast of a tyre imprint with a magnifying glass.

'How do they expect me to find tread marks on a bald tyre?' he wondered aloud.

'Because you're the best, Bernie, that's why.'

Bernie set down both the cast and the magnifying glass, then eyed Jesse suspiciously. 'That sounds like a prelude to a request for a favour if ever I've heard one.'

'Uh . . . yeah, well, right you are.'

'What's it this time, Mach? A dog-hair you want analysed to find out who's chewing your morning paper? You want me to run tests on a lipstick on your collar and give you a brand name so you can buy her a present for your next date? What?'

'Actually, Bernie,' Jesse said, 'I was just wondering if you could lift a set of fingerprints for me.'

Bernie scratched his beard. 'That's too easy, Mach. What's the catch? I have to dust an entire football stadium, right?'

Jesse shook his head. 'County Morgue.'

'A stiff?' Bernie went back to inspecting the tyre imprint. 'No way. Forget it, Mach. Lift your own prints.'

'Bernie—'

'Yeah, that's my name, all right,' Bernie said. 'I'm Bernie, not Igor. Dead bodies aren't my thing. Do it yourself.'

'I can't do it alone.'

'Why not?'

'It's a long story.'

'Aren't they all?' Bernie tried to ignore Jesse and concentrate on his work, but Jesse wouldn't leave. Finally Bernie looked up and said, 'Okay, okay. Look, if you get the prints and bring them to me, I'll run a make on them. But I'm not busting into the Morgue. You'll have to find another sucker to help you out on that front. . . .'

TWENTY-NINE

'I won't do it!'

Norman shook his head emphatically as he circled around Street Hawk, making necessary adjustments according to various readings on the bike's high-performance calibrator.

'Norman, come on,' Jesse badgered. 'I can't pull this off on my own. I already explained that to you. Look, aren't we a team? A two-man operation? That's what you're always telling me. . . .'

'That's right,' Norman agreed. 'Only the way it works is that we're a team with you on the bike and me here supervising. It has nothing to do with these Hardy Boy antics you're proposing. Besides, I'm going shopping after I'm through here. I want to buy a new shirt for the concert.'

'I've got plenty of new shirts,' Jesse bartered. 'I'll loan you one of mine.'

'Forget it, Mach. The answer is no. End of discussion.' Norman went over to a nearby bench and carefully picked up a small missile that was roughly the size of a submarine sandwich. He took it over to Street Hawk and gently slipped it into the bike's front launch bay, telling Jesse,

'Now, if you don't mind, I have to recalibrate your CD-two launcher to accommodate this little baby here. . . .'

'That's some baby,' Jesse said. 'What is it?'

'That heat-seeking missile I was telling you about the other day. I was hoping you'd try it out during a test run tonight.'

'I'm not scheduled for a run tonight, Norman.'

'I know,' Norman said, 'but it'd be a big help. The agency is on my back to get some trial results, and I've already been putting them off for more than a week as it is.'

'I see. . . .' Jesse smiled as he patted the launch bay. 'Gee, Norman, it sounds to me like you're asking me a favour.' .

Norman saw the gleam in Jesse's eye and realized he was trapped. 'Oh, come on, Mach, it's hardly a fair trade-off. You're asking me to illegally infiltrate a morgue, for crying out loud!'

Jesse countered, 'And every time I put on that riding suit and take Street Hawk on a test run, I'm a wanted man! Think about it, Norman. . . .'

Norman turned away from Jesse and wiped his hands on a towel. When he was done with it, he wadded it up and threw it into a hamper across the room, then sighed with exasperation. 'Okay, Jesse. Fair is fair. When do you want to make this raid on the morgue?'

'Attaboy!' Jesse said, heading for the door and holding it open for Norman. 'Let's go. No time like the present, I always say.'

'I should have known. . . .'

Jesse had borrowed a few things from Bernie, including a pair of official-looking white smocks and lab jackets. Before piling into his Mustang, he and Norman suited up.

'Okay, the plan's very simple,' Jesse said, going on to explain the details as he drove across town to the Morgue, an appropriately forbidding-looking building half-hidden in the shadows of nearby skyscrapers.

'I can't believe I'm actually going through with this,' Norman muttered as he got out of the car after Jesse had parked. 'I mean, we aren't even in the Morgue yet and already my skin's starting to crawl.'

'Norman, will you relax?' Jesse said as they headed up the walk to the side entrance. 'You're going to blow our cover if you don't watch it. Remember, you have to act like you do this for a living. Take it in your stride.'

'I'm trying, dammit!' Norman complained. 'I just can't help feeling like I'm an extra in some kind of a Frankenstein movie.'

'You'll get over it.' Before they entered the Morgue, Jesse pulled a small leather case out of his lab jacket and handed it to Norman. 'Here. You know how to use this?'

Norman stared at the case as if it were something from outer space. As he pried open the lid, he mumbled, 'Use it? I don't even know what it is!'

'It's a fingerprint kit.'

'I should have guessed. How does it work?'

'Very simply,' Jesse explained. 'Just roll each of his fingers firmly across the pad. That's all there is to it.'

'Can I practice once on you?'

'We don't have time.' Jesse opened the door and let Norman enter the Morgue ahead of him. It was quiet inside, and their footsteps echoed eerily off the walls of the corridor.

'I won't do anything illegal,' Norman insisted.

'Norman, we're only after fingerprints, not spare body parts,' Jesse said. 'Just follow my lead and be ready to carry out the plan. Keep cool and everything will come off like clockwork.'

Rounding the corner, the duo came upon their first obstacle in the form of a bored attendant who was manning the front desk, thumbing through a copy of 'The Sporting News' to keep himself busy. Norman seemed slightly relieved to see that the attendant was so young and unintimidating.

'Hi,' Jesse called out as he approached the desk. 'Gimble and Gann Mortuary to pick up John Burton.'

The attendant set down his paper and frowned as he scanned a clipboard on the desk. 'Burton . . . Burton . . . I hate to tell you this, but we don't have any Burtons listed here. You're going to have to backtrack through Forensic.'

Jesse smiled sheepishly, as if embarrassed to make a confession. 'Listen, this is our first time out. Do you think you could maybe help me straighten this out?'

The attendant clearly was impressed at being put in a position of being the man in charge. He set aside the clipboard and rose from his seat, taking on an officious manner no doubt modelled after one of his superiors. 'Come on, I'll take you down,' he told Jesse.

Before following the other man down the hall, Jesse winked at his cohort and said, 'Norman, why don't you call Mr Gimble and tell him we're going to be held up a while?'

'There's a pay phone just down the hall,' the attendant told Norman.

'Thanks,' Norman said, fishing through his pockets for spare change. He started for the phone, but as soon as Jesse and the attendant had wandered out of sight, he made a quick U-turn, backtracking to the main desk. Scanning through the listings on the clipboard, Norman was able to discover that the body of the man purported to be Jake Cannon was in box number fifty-seven in the freezer section of the Morgue.

It took Norman a few minutes to track down the basement area he was looking for, and a few seconds after that to summon up his nerve before going inside to carry out his part in Jesse's plot. He'd seen freezer rooms on television in reruns of *Quincy*, but that exposure was inadequate in preparing him for the actual experience of tracking down a particular box and pulling it out to reveal a wrapped corpse lying on a cold slab. He fought back a faintheadedness as he fumbled with the wrap, getting the dead man's hand free so that he could lift his fingerprints with the kit Jesse had given him. He didn't waste any time completing this task, and as soon as he was back in the warmer air of the outside corridor, Norman let out a long, deep breath of thanksgiving before hurrying back to the main lobby.

Only a few seconds after Norman had returned, Jesse and the attendant emerged from the other hallway, caught up in conversation.

'I can't figure it out,' the attendant was saying. 'Let's check Receiving. Maybe he's a new arrival.'

Jesse glanced over at Norman, who flashed him a thumbs-up signal, then told the attendant, 'We really appreciate this. You could be saving our jobs.'

'No problem.'

'I just got off the phone with Mr Gimble,' Norman told the other men as they joined him. 'He says we made a mistake . . . wrong morgue.'

The attendant made a perplexed face. 'Are you sure? We're the only morgue in town.'

'Maybe he meant the wrong town,' Jesse said, heading for the exit. 'Look, we won't take up any more of your time. Sorry for sending you on a wild goose chase.'

The attendant shrugged. By the time Jesse and Norman had turned the corner, he was already flipping back through his paper.

'I just have to drop the prints off at Bernie's, then I'll be all yours,' Jesse promised Norman as he took the fingerprint kit. 'By the way, you did a nice job. Oscar material all the way.'

'You think so?' Norman said, genuinely flattered. 'I mean, this was my first assignment in the field.'

'Norman, you're a natural. Field assignments, dates with blonde bombshells . . . you're going to turn into a regular James Bond on me if you don't watch it, pal.'

Norman waved away the praise, but the prideful glow in his cheeks suggested that he was taking some of it to heart. As he joined Jesse in the Mustang, he speculated, 'Boy, wouldn't she flip if she really knew what I did for a living. . . .'

THIRTY

A glorious sunset surrendered its colours to the creeping blackness of night, and soon a cloudless sky lorded over the city. At the Long Beach National Guard Armoury, a pot-bellied security guard fiddled with the antenna of his portable television, trying to pick up the ballgame. He was at his post in a booth stationed at the main entrance of the Armoury, and after rummaging around the small cubicle, he was able to track down a chunk of high-gauge wire that collaborated nicely with the antenna in bringing the picture into a clear focus. Satisfied with his handiwork, the guard was about to heft his bulk onto a padded stool when a set of headlights raked the booth with their bright shafts of light.

'Ahh, wouldn't ya know it,' the guard grumbled as he adjusted his holster and then squeezed out of the guard booth to confront the brown station wagon that had pulled to a stop in front of the main gates.

Jake Cannon was driving the wagon. With him was one of the commandos who had helped him escape the day before. They were both dressed in military outfits, and Cannon had an ID badge and forged order papers he'd put together during the afternoon.

'Evenin', officer,' Cannon told the guard as he rolled down his window and presented his identification. 'We got a call from Corporal Roberts to come down and check into a few discrepancies in the last ammo shipment that came in here.'

'That so?' the guard said as he skimmed over Cannon's papers. 'Well, this looks fine to me. Only problem is I don't have any orders from Corporal Roberts coinciding with this. You're going to have to wait a second while I call him.'

'Fine,' Cannon replied calmly. When the guard handed the papers back, Cannon didn't get a firm grip on them, and several sheets fluttered down to the ground. 'Sorry about that, officer. . . .'

'No problem.' The guard leaned over to retrieve the fallen papers. Cannon took immediate advantage of the planned distraction, whipping open his door with so much force that the security officer was knocked off his feet. With cat-like agility, Cannon bounded out of the car and knocked the guard unconscious with the butt of his revolver. Cannon's accomplice slid over behind the wheel, and when Cannon had helped himself to the guard's keys and opened the gates, the commando drove into the compound and waited for Cannon to circle around to the passenger's side and get back in before continuing to the Armoury's ammunition storage facilities, located four hundred yards away, next to an open-spaced training field.

'Okay,' Cannon told his partner, 'pull around to the rear loading area and then back in.'

Cannon jumped out of the station wagon and proceeded on foot to the back doors of the warehouse, carrying his revolver in one hand and a pair of bolt cutters in the other. He encountered no other Armoury personnel, and by the time the station wagon had been backed up to the loading dock, Cannon had snapped the lock on the doors and swung them open. An alarm sounded, but Cannon quickly tracked down the control box and snipped its wires in a matter of seconds.

'They might think it's a false alarm, but let's not take any chances,' he told the commando. 'Let's load up quick and get out of here.'

*

Jesse was headed back from the rugged wilds of the San Gabriel Mountains, where he'd encountered the Highway Patrol before. He had in mind a perfectly secluded area for making the test run with Street Hawk's new heat-seeking missile. However, as he was just exiting from the Foothill Freeway in Duarte and preparing to head north, Norman alerted him to a sudden change in plans.

'Mach, I'm receiving a military alert. Somebody's hitting an armoury!'

'Where?' Jesse asked.

'Behind you, down in Long Beach. That's a long way from where you are. You want to try for it?'

'You bet,' Jesse said, feeling a surge of adrenalin course through him. 'I'm right near the Santa Fe Flood Basin, so let me hang a cookie and drop into the drainage channel so we can do some serious hyperthrust.'

'You want to translate that for me?' Norman asked. 'What's a cookie?'

'One of these. . . .'

Jesse applied the airfoils and firmed his grip on Street Hawk as the bike made a logic-defying one hundred and eighty degree turn in the space of a few yards. Now heading south on the San Gabriel River Freeway, Jesse looked for the likeliest spot to jump the barrier surrounding the Santa Fe dam and enter the flood basin.

'That was an uncalled for U-Turn,' Norman scolded. 'You could have wiped out . . .'

'True, but I didn't. Hang on, sports fans,' Jesse said as he left the road and applied vertical lift to leap over the fence surrounding the dam. 'I hope you fixed that hairline fracture on the Magnum spoke, Norman.'

'I did . . . and thanks for landing correctly, anyway.'

'My pleasure.'

The flood basin was bone dry, as it was most of the year, and Jesse had no problem crossing the hard-packed ground to the cement-lined runoff channel that ran all the way from the dam to Long Beach Harbour. Aside from strewn litter and a few pernicious weeds that had grown up through cracks in the concrete, the channel was tailor-made for a motorcycle travelling at speeds of between two and three hundred miles an hour. Los Angeles was comprised of innumerable smaller cities huddling next to one another, and Jesse raced past many of them on his way to Long Beach. Irwindale, Baldwin Park, El Monte, Industry, Pico Rivera, Sante Fe Springs, Downey, Norwalk, Bellflower, Cerritos, Lakewood—they all went by in a blur as he sped down the concrete chute, gracefully banking on the curves and riding hard down the straightaways.

'Since our prints of that stiff in the Morgue proved Cannon didn't die in the fire,' Jesse said as he rode, 'how much do you want to bet our man's behind this raid on the Armoury?'

'You think it's him?' Norman queried.

'It's a natural, Norman. I already told you that the guards at Simone Prevera's mansion looked like the same commandos who sprang Cannon from the prison van. The way I put it together, he's going to be playing Che Guevara soon and he's probably busting into the Armoury to load up on popguns.'

Jake Cannon already had his popguns. He'd come to the Armoury looking for a wider range of artillery and munitions. One didn't storm a naval yard with six-shooters, he reasoned, and as he and the commando transferred one last load into the back of their station wagon, he was pleased with the result of their raid.

'This should do the trick for us,' he said, slamming the rear tailgate of the vehicle. As he was heading for the front seat, however, his look of contentment abruptly changed to one of concern. The relative quiet of the Armoury had been suddenly disrupted by the howl of sirens, and now two police cruisers were bounding across the training field toward the warehouse, beacons flashing wildly.

Cannon rushed back to the rear of the wagon and hauled out an Uzi submachine gun. His partner had already grabbed one, and they both sprayed bursts of gunfire at the approaching patrol cars. The lead vehicle took a few direct hits to its front tyres and skidded out of control, ramming into a high-pitched embankment and rolling over on its side. The second squad car brodied to a quick halt and two officers jumped out, returning fire.

Jesse screeched onto the scene several moments later. Norman enhanced the visor image of the confrontation between the police and the men behind the brown station wagon, which Jesse quickly recognized as the same getaway vehicle that had been used to spirit away Cannon following the sabotage of the police van.

'It's him, all right,' Norman concurred, seeing the relayed view of Cannon and the commando on his monitor screen miles away. 'Careful, Jesse.'

Norman's warning came seconds before Cannon spotted Street Hawk and began directing his fire at the bike. Jesse outraced the stream of bullets as he circled about so that the overturned police vehicle lay between him and the station wagon.

Cannon quickly slapped a fresh cartridge into his Uzi and told the commando, 'Take the wheel and be ready to swing around the warehouse. We'll go for the side exit!'

As the commando ceased firing and got back in the car, Cannon took careful aim at the disabled squad car's engine compartment. As he'd guessed, there was a gas leak under the hood, and his gunfire managed to ignite a fast-spreading blaze that soon engulfed the entire vehicle, trapping the officers inside.

When the other two policemen quit firing at Cannon and rushed to aid their comrades, Cannon leapt back in the station wagon. The commando floored the accelerator and drove off, narrowly missing the edge of the warehouse as he cut the corner.

Jesse began to give chase, but when he realized that the doors of the burning police cruiser were jammed shut and its trapped officers were beginning to shout in fear, he braked to a stop, letting the station wagon get away. As he watched the other officers struggle futilely to get close to the inferno, Jesse heard Norman calling out, 'Train the particle beam on the doors . . . half power. Hurry!'

Jesse followed Norman's advice, taking careful aim with

the motorcycle's sophisticated turret gun, then unleashing an energized beam that rocked the nearest door of the overturned vehicle until it shook free, allowing the officers inside to struggle out through the veil of flames, coughing and bruised from the crash but otherwise unharmed. Rather than stay around to make sure everything was okay, Jesse quickly set out in pursuit of the getaway station wagon. It was too late, however, because the side exit was only a hundred yards away from the warehouse, and the vehicle had already crashed through the barrier and reached the city streets.

THIRTY-ONE

The following morning, Jesse dropped by the Street Hawk Command Centre on his way to work. He found Norman sitting at the master control module, sipping coffee and reading through the paper as the computers whirred behind him.

'You look terrible,' Norman said as he set aside the paper. 'Didn't you get any sleep at all last night, Mach?'

Jesse shook his head. He had dark circles under his eyes, which were bloodshot and void of their usual vitality. 'You know how they say that if you can't sleep you should try counting sheep? Well, all I could do was count the number of times Cannon's got away from me.'

'You shouldn't be blaming yourself.'

'Yeah, that's easy to say. Do you have any more coffee?'

Norman nodded in the direction of a coffee maker on the stand next to the exercise room. 'Help yourself. It's decaffeinated, though.'

'Figures,' Jesse said, pouring himself a cup. 'Any word on that cop who took the worst burns last night?'

'I'm accessing the hospital computer right now,' Norman said, turning his attention back to the keyboard in front of him. 'It takes a while.'

As he waited for his coffee to cool down, Jesse snatched the morning paper from the console and looked over the front page story, which featured a picture of the burning police cruiser next to the Armoury warehouse.

'I can't believe the car didn't blow up sooner than it did,' he commented.

'Here's the report,' Norman said, looking up at the monitor, which listed medical statuses of burn victims at the Sherman Oaks Burn Unit. He tracked down the name of the officer involved in the altercation at the Armoury. 'They've still got him down as critical. I think that's standard procedure, though, on somebody who was burned as much as—'

'Damn!' Jesse interrupted, rattling the newspaper as he held it up closer to his face. 'It says here that a security guard at the Armoury was killed when Cannon broke in!'

'I know,' Norman murmured.

'When?'

'What?'

'When did you know?' Jesse demanded. 'Did you know about this last night?'

Norman sighed as he nodded his head. 'Jesse, I didn't want to upset you any more than you already were. Look, it happened before we even knew there was a break-in. . . .'

Jesse crumpled up the paper and threw it on the floor. 'If I had made sure that Cannon stayed behind bars, there wouldn't have even been a break-in, Norman!'

'You did your best.'

'Yeah, but my best wasn't good enough, was it?' Jesse said. 'How many people has Cannon killed or injured in just the past few days, all because I wasn't able to—'

'Jesse, knock it off!' Norman snapped. He moved away from the computers and confronted his partner. 'Wallowing in self-pity isn't going to bring back the dead or help the wounded, so just give it a rest, would you?'

Jesse glared contemptuously at Norman, but said nothing. His rage passed, but not his frustration. After quickly downing the rest of his coffee, Jesse moved to leave the room.

'Where are you going?' Norman asked him.

'To work,' Jesse said. 'To see if I can't get a new lead on Cannon and take him off the streets once and for all.'

'Don't do anything stupid.'

'I won't, don't worry,' Jesse said.

'Is there anything I can do to help?'

'Yeah, as a matter of fact. There was no mention in the paper about what Cannon swiped at the Armoury. Do you think you can get some info on it for me? It might give us a chance to figure out his next move.'

'Consider it done. If you can wait, I'll do it right now.'

'I'd appreciate it.'

Norman cleared his computers, then programmed a series of requests to various sources he hoped might be able to provide him with the information he was seeking. No word had been provided to the media yet, it turned out, but an inventory had been taken of the raided warehouse, and the results showed up when Norman queried the National Guard's computers. He passed along the news to Jesse.

'For the most part he went after the heaviest artillery he could fit into the back of a station wagon. Uzi submachine guns, a couple M-210s, four M-90s and a LAWS rocket. It's not enough to wage a war with, but it sure could make for one hell of an assault. . . .'

THIRTY-TWO

Unlike Norman's pot of generic decaffeinated coffee, Simone's morning cup of brown brew came from the finest South American beans, given to her as a gift from an acquaintance in San Leandro. She sipped the coffee slowly, enjoying its rich taste and aroma as she stared out at her villa courtyard, where a gardener was trimming back the bougainvillea and sorting some of the more flowery cut branches into a large crystal vase resting on the rattan table next to him. The morning sun fell on her face with its welcome warmth, reminding her vaguely of outdoor breakfasts she used to enjoy in her native country, before the fall. To think that soon she might once again be able to indulge in those luxurious mornings gave her an inner thrill that almost made her shake with anticipation. Granted, this was a nice life she had laid out before her in Malibu, but there were too many things missing. More than anything, she missed the power. It was one thing to have control over a loyal household staff and a small band of men willing to do her bidding for her here in the States, but it was quite another to have an entire country under her domain. No, she would not feel truly fulfilled until she could once again proclaim to the world that she was Queen Simone, sole monarch and absolute ruler of San Leandro.

Jake Cannon, on the other hand, had ideas of his own. As he emerged from the bedroom he had shared with Simone the night before, he walked with a contented swagger, pleased with the way things were beginning to turn out for him. He'd been through hell and high water the past couple of days, but that was all behind him. He'd done his time kowtowing to other people, always acting on their orders because it was in the nature of being a mercenary. But now things were going to change. Thanks to Simone, he was vaulting to a position of power that he had only dared to dream about before. The only obstacle he foresaw was establishing command, and after the good time he'd shown Simone last night, he was sure that he'd have no problem convincing her that it was in her best interests to acknowledge his dominance.

Cannon squinted as he stepped outside into the glare of the morning sun, then strolled over to where Simone was sitting.

'Morning, gorgeous,' he greeted her, giving her a kiss before pulling up a chaise-longue and sitting next to her.

'Sleep well?' Simone asked him.

'Like a baby. And you? You must have been exhausted after the time we had, huh?'

Simone smiled stiffly. 'I slept well enough, thank you.'

'No need to thank me,' Cannon chuckled. 'I had a pretty decent time myself.'

'I'm glad.'

Cannon noted the table next to Simone and frowned. 'Service for one?'

'I like to eat breakfast alone,' Simone said simply, setting down her mug of coffee and applying butter to what was left of her roll.

'I don't,' Cannon said, snapping his fingers to get the attention of a butler who stood off to the edge of the patio. 'Hey, scare me up some scrambled eggs, rye toast, and as much bacon as you've got. I'm starved!'

The butler looked questioningly at Simone, who hesitated

a moment before nodding. Once the man had moved out of earshot, Simone turned to Cannon and said, 'In the future, I would appreciate it if you would respect my wishes, Jake. I distinctly said that I preferred to have my breakfast alone.'

'Yeah, yeah, I heard.' Cannon lit up a cigarette and tossed the match onto the bricks of the patio. 'You know, Simone, the trouble with you is you're spoiled. El Presidente let you do too many things on your own.'

'Oh, is that a fact?' Simone said, instinctively on her guard. 'Funny, I don't remember you complaining back then.'

'It was a different story back then, Simone. It's a whole new ballgame now,' Cannon told her. 'And I'm not just a designated hitter any more. Now I see myself more along the lines of a player-manager.'

'Meaning . . .?'

'Meaning I'm not your gutless husband, rest his pathetic soul.' When Simone recoiled, Cannon added, 'Come on, don't act so offended. You couldn't stand him. Admit it. We would have gotten together a whole lot sooner if you hadn't been so afraid of him. Well, he's out of the picture now, and I'm the new man in charge.'

Simone saw Cannon flicking ash on the brick and handed him an ashtray, fighting to keep her cool. 'It's nice to see that you're showing so much initiative, Jake, but you mustn't forget our arrangement. I plan to be sole ruler of San Leandro. As my righthand man, you will have countless privileges and your share of power, but it is I who will be in charge. . . .'

The butler was returning with a place setting to add to the table. Cannon smiled through a mouthful of smoke, telling Simone, 'We'll see about that, Simone. I think it'd be best to discuss this matter at a more convenient time . . . say tonight, between silk sheets?'

Simone rose from her chair. 'Perhaps, Jake. Now, if you'll excuse me a moment, I'll go get us some more coffee. I like to make it myself, you know.'

'Yes, I remember. . . .'

As Simone left the patio and began to cross the courtyard

toward the kitchen, she signalled for her bodyguard, a lean, hard-looking San Leandran named Jorge, who had been lingering in the background. He fell in beside her and they walked together a few steps. When she was sure that they were beyond Cannon's earshot, Simone told Jorge, 'Once Mr Cannon has helped us to achieve our aims, I want him killed. Is that understood?'

Jorge nodded, curling his lips upward with the hint of a smile. 'Yes, ma'am.'

Simone glanced over her shoulder, watching Cannon grind the butt of his cigarette against the patio brick with the heel of his shoe. 'And when you kill him, Jorge,' she added, 'I want to be there. . . .'

THIRTY-THREE

The convict who had died in the jail kitchen blaze turned out to be a petty thief named William Blandon. At the police station, Jesse put a call through to Blandon's most recent parole officer, who checked his records and reported an address in North Hollywood as the dead man's last known residence. As Jesse was hanging up the phone, he saw Altobelli heading toward his desk. From the look on the Commander's face, Jesse didn't think that the trip to the Morgue had yet come to his boss' attention. Altobelli had a look of displeasure, but it was his normal working expression, not one distorted by a surprise aggravation.

'I've got Rachel working on the Street Hawk case, too, Mach,' the Commander informed Jesse. 'If you ever take the time to run into her, the two of you might put your heads together and see if you can't help one another and cut down on duplicate work, got it? I want results on this thing, A.S.A.P. . . .'

'Will do, chief.' Jesse folded the sheet of paper with Blandon's address and slipped it in his pocket as he left the squad room. Taking the elevator to Rachel's floor, he tracked her down in her office, where she was busy typing up a report. When she glanced up and saw Jesse, she made a face and quickly turned back to her work.

'Rachel, I've been looking all over for you.'

'Save it, Mach. I can smell a tall tale from a mile away.' Rachel ran her fingers across the typewriter keyboard. 'I suppose Altobelli told you I'm fed up with the way you handle your duties. Or should I say, the way you *don't* handle your duties.'

'Yeah, and I want to apologize,' Jesse said. 'Look, what have you come up with on Street Hawk so far? Any strong leads?'

Rachel stopped typing long enough to give Jesse a look of cool disdain. 'I'll send you a memo.'

'Look, let me make things up to you, Rachel,' Jesse said, thinking fast. 'I know a few custom bike shops up in the east end of the Valley. I could go up there and ask around, see if anyone knows somebody who might have done some experimental customizing along the lines of the special tricks that this Street Hawk has been pulling with his bike. It seems like a natural place to start.'

'Okay, Jesse,' Rachel replied glibly. 'Go ahead, leave the office for the rest of the day. That's what you're good at. You can handle the technical end of the investigation. I'll concentrate on trying to get a bead on the rider.'

'You mean psychological profile and whatnot?'

'Let me worry about that, okay, Jesse?' Rachel resumed her typing. 'Now just leave me alone and do your thing. I've got plenty of work to do here.'

Jesse grinned to himself as he left the office and took the stairs down to the parking lot. He'd be curious to find out what Rachel might come up with in terms of a speculative character sketch of the man she thought to be responsible for Street Hawk's current notoriety throughout the city. If she only knew she was working with him. . . .

It was a forty-minute drive to North Hollywood, one of the older communities that made up the heavily-populated San Fernando Valley. The air above the city was loud with the sound of aircraft coming in for landings at nearby Burbank Airport. It was mid-morning, and traffic was light, enabling Jesse to drive slowly as he got his bearings and tracked down the address he was seeking.

William Blandon's last civilian residence was a small, one-story adobe house squatting on a small parcel of hard-soiled land near the intersection of Colfax and Lankersheim. Ankle-high grass rose from the lawn in random patches, sharing space with clover, dandelions, and a handful of other weeds. A scattering of untrimmed junipers dotted the periphery of the yard and stood out in front of the house like overgrown pom-poms waiting for someone to pick them up and shake them.

Jesse parked his Mustang and strode up the front walk. The main door was open, and Jesse glanced in through the outer screen door as he rang the doorbell and called out, 'Anybody home?'

There was no answer, but Jesse could smell chicken soup cooking in the kitchen and he saw the flickering light of a television set reflecting off the wall of the living room. He rang the doorbell a second time, and when still no one came to the door, he quietly let himself in.

'Hello?' His voice bounded off the walls, sounding loud in comparison to the low drone of the television. Jesse peered into the den and saw that no one was watching the set. He left it on and proceeded cautiously down the hallway. Perhaps there was someone out in the back yard, he thought to himself, trying to fight back the paranoia that was making its presence known in his system.

Reaching the master bedroom, Jesse stepped around the heaps of rumpled clothes that dotted the worn carpet like islands on a polluted sea. Most of the clothes were dresses, blouses, and skirts, which Jesse quickly surmised belonged to the woman pictured in a framed photograph on the chest of drawers. There was a man in the picture, too, and Jesse was amazed at the striking resemblance between William Blandon and Jake Cannon. No wonder it had been so easy for the one to stand in for the other. He picked the photo up for a closer look.

'Put it down,' a woman's voice suddenly cut through the silence in the bedroom.

Jesse slowly lowered the picture as he turned around. The woman in the photograph was now standing in the doorway, holding a .357 Magnum in front of her. It wasn't clear if she knew how to use it, but her finger rested on the trigger and that was all Jesse needed to see.

'Okay,' he said, putting the photo back on the chest of drawers. 'Now will you point that gun somewhere else, please? I'm a cop.'

'Try again, pretty boy.' The woman was only in her mid-twenties, but she had a tired look about her—the look of someone who had put all their money on a far-fetched dream and watched it fade before their eyes, leaving them hurt and angry.

'I've got identification,' Jesse insisted.

'Show me.' When Jesse started reaching for his coat the woman pulled back the hammer on her gun and snapped. 'Make it real slow. Don't make me shoot you.'

Jesse removed his badge and took a step forward so he could hand it to her. When she turned to look at it, Jesse lashed out with his right foot, catching the woman with a karate kick that knocked the gun from her hand. She tried to retrieve it, but Jesse got to it first. 'Sorry I had to do that, ma'am, but you were making me nervous.'

'Okay, so you're a tough guy,' the woman sniffed. 'It isn't loaded, anyway. Look, if you're looking for Willie, he ain't here.'

'Is he your boyfriend?' Jesse asked.

'Are you kidding? That yo-yo? No way.' She shook her head vigorously. 'I'm a friend of his sister. I'm just house-sitting here for the next six months, while Mr Good-For-Nothing does some time.'

Jesse made sure the gun wasn't loaded, then handed it back to the woman, breaking the news. 'You're going to be house-sitting a lot longer than that maybe.'

'What's that supposed to mean?'

'Willie's dead.'

The woman cocked her head to one side like a dog that hears one of the few words it understands. 'Dead? Willie? You can't be serious.'

'I'm afraid I am.' Jesse told her. 'I'll run it down for you if you're interested.'

The woman took a step back and leaned against the doorframe for support. Despite her avowed antipathy for William Brandon, the news of his death still came as a blow to her. 'How . . .' she whispered hoarsely.

'The way we figure it, he got himself talked into what he thought was a nice scam,' Jesse explained. 'Somebody offered him a lot of money to spend a little time in prison, only it didn't turn out that way. As soon as he'd served his purpose, he was killed and burned almost beyond recognition in a kitchen fire at the county jail.'

'I knew it. I knew it.' The woman shook her head and moved away from the doorframe. She was a few shades paler than normal but was otherwise under control. 'When he called me to sit the house for him and explained the deal, I told him it sounded like a scam. But he wouldn't listen to me. He was going nuts trying to make good on his parole, and he figured this would get him some quick cash, save him the trouble of having to find a decent job. I told him it didn't sound right.'

'Did he mention who made the offer to him?'

The woman thought it over. 'Some woman. Willie said she lived in some fancy beach house. She had a foreign sounding name. . . . I can't remember it, though. Peroba? Something like that . . .'

'Prevera?' Jesse said. 'Simone Prevera?'

'Yeah, that's it. You know her?'

'You might say that.' Jesse took a business card from his pocket and gave it to the woman, asking her, 'Would you be willing to testify in court about Simone Prevera making that offer to Willie?'

'Maybe . . . yeah, sure I would. Willie was a jerk, but he didn't deserve to die because of it. . . .'

THIRTY-FOUR

After putting through a quick call to Norman, Jesse drove directly to Malibu. Norman had advised that the situation called for the use of Street Hawk, but Jesse said the Malibu area was too well-watched by the Highway Patrol. He didn't want to risk the need of a high-speed chase on a thoroughfare as congested as Pacific Coast Highway. Also, being in North Hollywood, he was already halfway to Malibu Canyon Drive, a winding road that passed through the stretch of Santa Monica Mountains that separated the valley from the coast.

Jesse arrived in Malibu just as a late-morning cloud cover had rolled in to do battle with the midday sun. Instead of trying to gain admittance to Simone's estate by way of the main gate, he drove his Mustang past the entrance and turned down a side road that bordered the west end of the property. He pulled off the street and parked close to the stone wall, then checked for traffic before bounding up onto the roof of his car and over the barrier. A thick growth of ivy cushioned his landing, and Jesse quickly ducked behind a nearby row of camellia bushes for cover. There were more than thirty of the colourful shrubs, forming a continuous hedge that allowed Jesse to advance close to the villa without being spotted. The plush lawn absorbed each step he made, and soon he was close enough to the elongated garage to see several of the commandos uncrating the weapons they had stolen from the Armoury. In addition to those items Norman had mentioned, Jesse could also identify a box of M-16s, an M-70 grenade launcher, and a crate of large-capacity fire extinguishers.

Simone and Cannon appeared moments later from the side of the main house. They walked along the row of camellias as they approached the commandos. Jesse had a clear view of Cannon, and the mere sight of the man's smug countenance filled him with a righteous fury.

'Are we ready?' Cannon asked the commandos when he reached the station wagon.

'Yes, sir.'

'Good, then we'll leave in a moment.' Cannon turned to Simone, who was looking over the trove of weapons in the back of the station wagon. 'I'd feel better if we were going down there in a tank, but I still don't think we'll have any problems.'

'I have every confidence in you, Jake.'

'That's what I like to hear.' Cannon glanced down at his watch. 'In a little over an hour, we're going to be on our way to being very rich.'

'And very powerful,' Simone added.

'That's right. And when I get back, we'll celebrate in style.'

'You mean when *we* get back,' Simone said. 'I'm going with you.'

Cannon laughed, 'Don't be ridiculous, Simone. You'd only get in the way.'

Simone took a quick step forward, meeting Cannon jaw to jaw. 'May I remind you, Jake, that I'm standing here today only because I took up an automatic rifle and fought my way to freedom during the overthrow of my country? I can take care of myself.'

'I'm sure you can,' Cannon relented, taking a step back from the woman.

'Fine. Then we will wait until I have changed into something more appropriate for storming a naval shipyard. I'll only need a couple of minutes.'

Jesse had been able to overhear the entire conversation, but before he could take any action regarding what he'd heard, there was a blur of motion to his immediate right. He instinctively tried to duck to one side, but he was still unable to avoid the stock of Jorge's automatic rifle, which slammed mercilessly into the side of his head. Fireworks went off inside Jesse's skull as he slumped to the ground, rendered unconscious by the blow.

'What's going on over there?' Cannon called out, plucking an Uzi from the back of the station wagon and whirling about to aim in the direction of the noises he had just heard behind the camellias.

'We have an intruder,' Jorge reported, standing on his tiptoes so that Cannon could see him. 'The man who was here before.'

Simone and Cannon passed through a gap in the shrub to join Jorge. Jesse was lying face-down on the grass, so Cannon turned him over with his toe, muttering, 'Well, well, if it isn't my old faithful sidekick.'

'You know him?' Simone said. 'He's the one who was asking about you.'

'Yeah, I know him.' Cannon aimed his submachine gun at Jesse's head. 'Nice of him to show up so I could show him my appreciation for the time we spent together.'

'Don't!' Simone said, pushing the weapon away so it was pointing at the grass instead. 'He could be more valuable to us alive.'

'I don't see how—'

'As insurance,' Simone explained. 'If we run into any difficulties at the shipyard, we can always say that we have a hostage being held somewhere else . . . a hostage who would die if we weren't allowed to go free.'

Cannon mulled it over. 'But we aren't going to have any difficulties. I say we get rid of him and take our chances.'

'I forbid it!' Simone declared. Behind her, Jorge made it

clear whose side he was on. Cannon met the other man's threatening gaze and eased his grip on the Uzi.

'All right, suit yourself,' he told Simone, turning to leave. 'Do what you want with him, but hurry it up. We leave in two minutes, with or without you!'

Simone told Jorge, 'Tie the prisoner up and put him in the garden shed. We'll tend to him when we get back. If we run into trouble in Long Beach, tell Manuel to be prepared to execute him if things don't go our way.'

Jorge nodded and crouched over to pick up Jesse's inert form. Simone hurried back to the main house, quickly changing into snug-fitting combat fatigues so that she looked less like a pampered aristocrat and more like a guerilla freedom fighter. She reached the station wagon just as Cannon had circled around and was getting ready to head off down the driveway. After she climbed into the back seat, Cannon continued to the main gate, which Manuel opened. The station wagon pulled out onto the main street and sped past the side road where Jesse's Mustang was parked. Behind the Mustang was a pickup truck carrying a one-horse trailer behind it. Crouched down low behind the wheel was Norman Tuttle, his features half-hidden beneath the brim of a straw cowboy hat.

THIRTY-FIVE

When Jesse came to, he found himself lying on his side in a storage shed the size of most garages. The smell of various fertilizers and soil amendments was overpowering, but he wasn't sure if it was the odour or the sharp throbbing of his skull that made him feel nauseous. He had no idea how long he'd been unconscious or how he'd gotten where he was, but when he quickly realized he was bound with heavy twine at the wrists and ankles, he had a fairly good idea of what had happened.

The enclosure was lit through an open window, and Jesse could see an arsenal of gardening tools mounted on the wall furthest from him. Another wall was lined with several types of lawn mowers and power edgers, and there was a side exit in addition to the larger rollaway door. Jesse squirmed toward the side door, mimicking a caterpillar by drawing his body into a crouch and then extending to gain ground. It was a painful, not to mention painstaking process, but he was able to drag himself several yards before the exertion became too much and he stopped, gasping for breath and closing his eyes in hopes of concentrating hard enough to will away the ache in his head.

'Why didn't I listen to Norman,' he groaned to himself.

When he opened his eyes, Jesse's gaze settled on one of the mowers close by. It was an old manual reel model, with a series of exposed blades. The blades looked blunt and rusted, but they posed Jesse's best chance for freedom. He wriggled over to the mower, then turned on his side and groped behind his back until he could feel the cold metal of the blades pressing against his binds.

'Come on, baby,' he wheezed through his teeth as he began moving his wrists back and forth across the blade. Occasionally he was forced to wince and hold back a cry of pain as he shifted too much one way and felt the mower blades scraping against his flesh, but for the most part he was able to concentrate the cutting action on the twine. Fibre by fibre, the rope weakened until finally Jesse was able to work his hands free. He sat up and quickly untied his ankles, then rubbed his chafed skin as he plotted his next move.

Outside the shed there was a sudden sound of footsteps on gravel, coming closer every second. Jesse rose to his feet and snatched a pair of hedge-trimming shears from the tool rack, then stealthily hurried to the side door. He flattened himself against the wall behind the door and waited.

The footsteps drew nearer and became more tentative, stopping finally outside the door. Jesse looked down and saw the knob slowly turning. He tightened his grip on the shears, and when the door opened inward, he moved into action. With his free arm, he launched a powerful right cross that reached around the door and caught the man entering the shed in the stomach, doubling him over. A gun clattered to the ground as Jesse tackled his would-be adversary and prepared to threaten him with the shears to keep him quiet. Something changed his mind, however.

'Norman!' Jesse gasped, seeing that he'd pinned down his partner. 'What the hell are you doing here?'

'I . . . I thought you might need some help,' Norman said, staring with horror at the hedge shears wavering in front of his face. 'Look, can you move those out of my way, Mach?'

'Yeah . . . sorry.' Jesse stepped back and helped Norman to his feet. 'I still can't believe you're here, but it's good to see you.'

'Well, maybe I've taken a liking to this field work,' Norman said, bending over to pick up the gun he'd dropped. 'I got this off the guy I knocked out on the way here.'

'Did you see anyone else?'

'There're a couple guards near the villa and another one by the front gate,' Norman said. 'I saw Cannon and the woman heading out with a few more men before I jumped the wall. Do you know where they were going?'

Jesse nodded, taking the gun from Norman. 'I've used one of these things more than you have. We have to make it out of here as quick as we can. They're off to the Navy's shipyard in Long Beach.'

'How come?'

'I'm not sure,' Jesse admitted. 'But they said something about a lot of money and they're going down there armed to the teeth. We have to stop them.'

'One thing at a time,' Norman said. 'For starters, let's make sure we can get out of here. I mean, it was no problem jumping the wall from the top of a car. Getting back over's going to be another thing.'

Jesse pointed over Norman's shoulder at a ladder hanging from a set of nails on the wall. 'That might come in handy. . . .'

They took the ladder down and carefully carried it out of the shed. Norman was able to carry it by himself, allowing Jesse to move ahead with the gun and make sure the way was clear. He came across the slumped form of Manuel, the estate's gardener, lying near some shrubs where Norman had decked him. Jesse could see that he was still breathing. He peered over the top of the shrub, locating the other guards posted on the property. Satisfied that they weren't looking his way, he signalled for Norman to join him. They reached the wall unnoticed, and the ladder reached up high enough for them to easily scale the barrier.

Once he'd landed on the other side, Jesse looked at the

truck and horse trailer parked behind his Mustang and asked Norman, 'Where'd you get that rig?'

'Oh, I've had it for a while,' Norman said. 'I've been too busy to use it for some time, but it sure can come in handy in a pinch.'

'Yeah, I guess so. But why don't you leave it here for now. We can make better time back to headquarters in the Mustang. I want to get on Street Hawk and . . . Norman, what *genius*!' Jesse gazed with wonder as Norman moved around and opened the back doors of the horse trailer, revealing a well-tethered Street Hawk and Jesse's riding suit, both ready and waiting for immediate use. . . .

THIRTY-SIX

A shore patrol Jeep rolled slowly along the periphery of the Navy Yard. The three officers inside the vehicle maintained their routine vigilance over the area, checking for suspicious activity. The driver stopped momentarily in front of a chain-link gate and waited for another of the men to get out and inspect the padlock securing this, one of several side service entrances to the yard. Satisfied that the area was secure, the officer got back in the Jeep and they headed off to the next stop on their rounds.

Cannon watched the Jeep through binoculars from inside the brown station wagon, which was parked a few hundred yards away, partially hidden between a trash dumpster and the shade of a warehouse. As he set aside the binoculars and started up the wagon, Cannon told the others, 'Okay, this is it. We have thirty-five minutes before the shore patrol returns. Let's be efficient.'

Simone was riding behind Cannon in the back seat, with an M-16 cradled in her lap. As the wagon pulled to a stop in front of the gate that had just been inspected by the shore officers, she got out and stood guard while one of the commandos applied bolt cutters to the padlock, snapping its loop as easily as the lock back at the Armoury. Cannon drove through as soon as the gate was opened, then idled until Simone and the commando were back in the vehicle before proceeding to the docks. After the wagon had been parked in a discreet, out of the way place, the infiltrators poured out and began removing their munitions from the back.

'What is that?' Simone asked as she watched Cannon remove a long wooden box the size of a small coffin.

Cannon grinned as he patted the box. 'This is my can opener. . . .'

As the group approached the ship, its signs of wear and obsolescence became increasingly clear. The carrier had been past its prime when it had been loaned to San Leandro several years ago, and little had been done to refurbish either the ship's interior or exterior. As the Navy had rightly determined, the best use for the vessel was as a prospective target during manoeuvres scheduled for later that afternoon.

It was decided that Simone and Jorge would remain on deck to stand guard while the others descended to the hold and followed directions on a set of blueprints of the carrier, showing the precise location of where the money had been concealed inside the ship's hull.

'Should be right here,' Cannon said, signalling for the others to stop. It was relatively dark in the hold, and he had to flash a light on the hull and look closely to see the seams that had been left following the hiding of the San Leandro fortune. Moving back, he pried the lid off the wooden box and removed the LAWS rocket launcher and its accompanying missile. As he began to assemble the weapon, he called over his shoulder, 'Set up a bulkhead for us to get behind, then put in your earplugs and be ready with the fire extinguishers. This sucker isn't really meant to be fired in such close quarters, so we might have a bit of a mess on our hands before we get to the money.'

One of the commandos wondered aloud, 'Wouldn't it be better just to torch the seams open?'

'Probably,' Cannon confessed, 'and if we had half a day instead of half an hour, that's more than likely the way we'd do it. However, we're in a rush, so let's not waste time second-guessing me . . . understood?'

The commandos all fell silent and applied their earplugs as Cannon readied the rocket launcher, then took up position behind the bulkhead. 'Say your prayers, boys,' he chortled as he fired off the rocket.

The ship shook slightly and the men felt as if they were trapped in the centre of a thundercloud as the rocket hit its mark and exploded with a resounding blast that was close to deafening even through the earplugs. The hold filled with a thick, acrid cloud of smoke which the men warily advanced through until they reached the section of hull that had taken the brunt of the explosion. A gaping hole stood out in the inner plating, smouldering at the edges with the glow of heat. Cannon waited until the fire extinguishers had been used to cool off the jagged orifice, then stepped forward and shone his light inside the cavity. A few feet down from where the rocket had hit, plastic-wrapped bundles of currency were stacked in neat piles, barely disturbed by either the elements or the effects of the explosion.

'I think we've just struck the motherlode,' Cannon wisecracked as he discarded his earplugs and reached in for the first load. Each bundle was roughly the size of a duffle bag, and he had no problem lifting them out of the niche and passing them along to the next man, who in turn transferred the load to the commando beside him, and so on until the currency had made its way up to the outer deck. From there, the group made use of two dollies to transport the money down a loading ramp to the station wagon. In all there were more than thirty of the bundles, each one worth nearly three-quarters of a million dollars at the current exchange rate.

'Still no one onto us,' Cannon observed as he supervised the unloading of the first shipment. He asked Simone, 'How loud was that explosion out here?'

'It was pretty muffled,' Simone said. 'I'm sure they are used to such loud sounds here.'

'Let's hope so.' Cannon stacked the last of the bundles into the back of the station wagon, then quickly counted them. 'Well, we're halfway home. One more trip back to the boat and we'll have it all. Damn, I can already imagine myself spending it. Oh, Simone, it's gonna be grand! I'll be living like a king!'

Simone nodded demurely. As they headed back to the gangplank, she slowed her step, falling behind the others. Coming beside Jorge, she told him, 'Once we're back up on the ship, I want Cannon killed and thrown overboard. Is that clear?'

Jorge nodded.

By the time Simone and Jorge had caught up with the others, the dollies were already being reloaded on the main deck. Cannon had his back turned to Simone as he headed up the human chain transferring the bundles onto the handcarts. When he turned around with the last bundle, Cannon found Jorge pointing an M-16 at his chest.

'What's the problem, Jorge?' Cannon said calmly.

'You are the problem, Jake,' Simone said, stepping next to her bodyguard. 'You are a greedy, conceited bastard. I thought perhaps I'd be able to use you effectively and see that you were adequately compensated for your troubles, but now I don't think you'd be satisfied. I'd always have to be on the watch, wondering when you were going to make your move against me. That's not the way I want to rule my country.'

'I should have known,' Cannon said, letting anger creep into his voice. 'So you're going to shoot me with that elephant gun? Is that it? Let me warn you . . . a rifle shot isn't apt to be confused for somebody plopping a heavy load on the dock, know what I mean? Pull that trigger and you'll never get out of this Yard with the cash.'

'Perhaps you're right, Jake.' Simone asked Jorge, 'Do you have your hunting knife with you?'

'Yes, ma'am.'

'Then slit Mr Cannon's throat and throw him to the fish. . . .'

When Jorge bent forward to reach for the knife strapped to his ankle, Cannon flicked his wrists as hard as he could, flinging the bundle of currency at his would-be assassin. Jorge was knocked off-balance, and by the time he recovered,

Cannon had grabbed Simone and pressed the barrel of his .380 Walther against the woman's side.

'Drop the rifle, Jorge, or your Queen is dead!'

Jorge hesitated, but he knew Cannon wasn't bluffing and he reluctantly set down the M-16. Behind him, the other commandos watched on, not sure what to do.

'Jake, stop it!' Simone pleaded. 'I can reconsider my—'

'Shut up!' Cannon yelled in Simone's ear. He told the other men, 'Put down your weapons and get below deck. If you all play your cards right, you might still have a chance to plan your little revolution . . . minus your twenty million bucks, of course.'

One by one, the revolutionaries dropped their guns and paraded past Cannon and Simone into the hatchway. Jorge was the last to go in, glaring at Cannon, who dragged Simone to the opening and shoved her in with the others.

'You swine!' she shouted back at Cannon.

'Goodbye, Simone,' Cannon said. 'You had your chance. Too bad you didn't know a good setup when it was staring you in the face.'

After he had slammed the hatch door and bolted it shut from the outside, Cannon picked up the last bundle and added it to the pile stacked on one of the dollies. He carefully guided the cart down the gangplank to the station wagon, which was starting to sag on its springs from the currency it was already carrying. The back of the vehicle was crammed full, so Cannon wheeled the dolly alongside the wagon and opened the front passenger's door, then began loading bundles onto the bucket seat. He'd only managed to stack three of the parcels when he was distracted by a distinctive mechanical hum sounding from the far end of the dock.

'You again!' Cannon roared, seeing that Jesse had just powered Street Hawk into view. Enraged, he assumed a quick firing stance and squeezed off five quick shots with his Walther.

Jesse had anticipated the gunshots, and he upended Street Hawk, lunging forward at a sharp angle on the bike's rear tyre, avoiding all five of the bullets.

Cannon climbed over the bundles on the front seat and slid behind the steering wheel. Jesse fired bursts from his .50 calibre machine guns at the station wagon, ripping holes in the vehicle's body but not preventing Cannon from driving off toward the nearest cluster of warehouses.

Jesse followed in quick pursuit, and as they approached the closest building, the two vehicles were racing side by side. When Cannon spotted Street Hawk out of the corner of his eye, he cranked his steering wheel sharply to one side, swerving into the bike's path. In order to avoid a collision, Jesse was forced to veer his own course and ride headlong into the warehouse, where a mess of strewn carts and storage crates created an even more difficult obstacle course to manoeuvre through.

Although Cannon had managed to shake Jesse off his tail for the moment, he did so at the expense of his own chances of a getaway. His sharp turn had put him on a direct collision course with a stack of loading skids, and because of the weight he was carrying, his brakes weren't responsive enough to prevent him from veering sideways into the skids, which tumbled down on the station wagon and shattered the front windshield. There was no way he could drive any further.

Furious, Cannon reached into the back seat for the M-70 grenade launcher, determined to rid himself of the man who had tormented him constantly since his arrival in Los Angeles. Once he had Street Hawk out of the way, he figured he could grab at least one bundle and make an escape on foot. Three-quarters of a million dollars could go a long way for a man on the run.

'I'm gonna love this,' he muttered to himself as he armed the launcher and took up a firing position close to the car, figuring his enemy would be coming back. He was able to hear the motorcycle making its way through the warehouse, then back out into the open. Bracing himself, Cannon peered through the sights of the launcher, waiting for Street Hawk to ride into its path.

As he cleared the warehouse, Jesse quickly looked from side to side, trying to spot Cannon. There was a fine layer of sawdust on the ground, and when he didn't see any tyre tracks, Jesse surmised that Cannon hadn't come this far. Circling around to the side of the warehouse, he was about to enter a maze of stacked skids and oversize storage containers when there was a sudden explosion to his left and a shower of wooden splinters rained on him as a crate the size of a mail truck was turned into a blaze of kindling by Cannon's grenade.

Jesse swung his bike around and spotted Cannon reloading the M-70 with another grenade.

'Okay, Cannon. If that's the way you want to play it.' Jesse put Street Hawk on idle and reached for the controls that operated the newly installed heat-seeking missile Norman had recently added to the bike's arsenal. 'I'm going to fight fire with fire. . . .'

A seemingly timeless moment lingered as the two foes faced off like modern-day descendants of gunslingers who had met on the streets at high noon to settle their differences. Instead of handguns, however, both men had their fingers on the triggers of weapons that could effectively annihilate the opposition.

Both men fired simultaneously. Cannon's shot was low, slamming into the asphalt thirty yards in front of Street Hawk but exploding with such a flourish that Jesse wasn't immediately able to see through the smoke and determine how close his missile had come to its mark. He shifted into first gear and slowly advanced through the low bank of smoke until he was finally able to make out the blazing hulk that had once been a brown station wagon. Loose currency floated in the air and littered the asphalt, but most of it had been destroyed when the missile had sought out the heated engine of the station wagon and added to the explosive force of the warhead.

Jake Cannon was sprawled out on the pavement, bleeding from countless shrapnel wounds and hanging on to a thread of consciousness. Jesse paused next to the beaten man and stared down at him, tempted to raise his helmet visor and let Cannon know who had brought him to justice. He resisted the temptation, however, and when the familiar sirens of the shore patrol announced the arrival of the authorities, Jesse opened up the throttle and sped away from the carnage left by the confrontation. His job was done. . . .

'As long as we're on the subject of women,' Norman said, 'aren't you going to ask me how my date went with Suzanne?'

'Oh, my God, I completely forgot, Norman! Yes, yes, tell all!'

Norman waited for the light to change, then eased down on the accelerator, turning onto the block where the police station was. 'Well, for starters, dinner rated a strong nine . . . excellent seafood, a good Chablis, delightful conversation.'

'Gee, that sounds almost as good as my pizza and draught beer over the six o'clock news,' Jesse teased.

'Ha ha, very funny. Now, as for the concert . . . another nine. Ah, Stravinsky like I'd never heard it before! Flawless arrangement, perfect tempo, top-notch acoustics.'

'Must have been those solos by Cupid that really made it for you, right?' Jesse said as they pulled into the station. 'Come on, let's get to the bottom line. How'd Suzanne rate?'

Norman's smile faded considerably. 'She fell asleep twice, then came down sick just before the encore, so we had to leave early.'

'Sorry to hear that, Norman.' When the pickup stopped in front of the station, Jesse opened the door but waited to get out. 'So I guess she gets a six, huh?'

The smile returned to Norman's face as quickly as it had disappeared. '*Au contraire, mon ami*,' he cooed in exaggerated French. 'She was so embarrassed, she demanded that I give her a chance to make up for everything. This weekend we're going to go to the ballet! Oh, I tell you, Jesse, this woman is a ten if there ever was one!'

Jesse reached over and patted Norman on the back. 'Congratulations, big guy. I didn't know you had it in you. Now, remember, I need you to pick me up at five so I can go get my car. For once I'm going to be forced into spending the entire day at the office. Rachel's going to faint!'

Jesse whistled as he entered the station and greeted his fellow officers on the way to the elevator. Tucked away in his coat pocket was a made-up list of customizing shops he supposedly checked out in the valley the day before. He ambled down to Rachel's office intent on flashing the sheet at her as a peace offering. However, it turned out that she wasn't in for a change. Jesse checked next door and found out that Rachel was meeting with a criminal psychologist down in the lounge.

'Oh, this I gotta see,' Jesse murmured, backtracking his way to the ground floor. On the way to the lounge, he ran into Commander Altobelli, who was staring bleakly at the front page of the morning paper as he waited for a cup of coffee in front of the vending machines.

'I hate him!!!' Altobelli was grumbling.

'Who's that, chief?'

'Who do you think, Mach!' Altobelli showed Jesse the front headlines, which declared: 'Street Hawk Overthrows Revolutionaries'.

'Oh,' Jesse said. 'Him.'

'Yes, *him*!' Altobelli grabbed his coffee and tossed the paper aside. Jesse picked it up and read through it as he made his way to the lounge, where he found Rachel chatting over coffee with an officious-looking young man who looked like he had aspirations of being a Sigmund Freud lookalike when he grew up.

'Hi, Rachel,' Jesse said as he joined them. 'Need me for anything here?'

'No, thanks,' Rachel responded coolly. 'I have everything under control. Jesse, this is Dr Gordon Pipps, a leading criminal psychologist. Dr Pipps, Jesse Mach, one of my cohorts . . . "part-time".'

'Pleased to meet you,' Jesse said, shaking Pipps' clammy hand. Dropping the paper nonchalantly on the table, he asked Rachel, 'See the headlines today? Our mystery guest has signed in again, so it seems.'

'Oh, I doubt that he'll be a mystery for long,' Rachel said

with an air of self-confidence. 'Now we have a bead on his psychological profile, it'll help our search for him immensely.'

'Oh, yeah?' Jesse said, his curiosity piqued. 'What's the lowdown?'

Rachel explained, 'We're convinced . . . Dr Pipps and I . . . that Street Hawk is suffering from an acute schizophrenic neurosis, induced by severe pre-adolescent trauma.'

Dr Pipps nodded benevolently in agreement with the analysis.

'Sounds pretty heavy,' Jesse said, trying to keep a straight face. 'But, what the heck, nobody's perfect, right. . .?'